SHADES OF LIGHT

SHADES OF LIGHT

THE HIDDEN MAGIC CHRONICLES

JUSTIN SLOAN

MICHAEL ANDERLE

DEDICATION

From Justin

To Ugulay, Verona and Brendan Sloan

From Michael

To Family, Friends and
Those Who Love
To Read.
May We All Enjoy Grace
To Live The Life We Are
Called.

DON'T MISS OUR NEW RELEASES

Join the LMBPN email list to be notified of new releases and special promotions (which happen often) by following this link:

http://lmbpn.com/email/

LMBPN Publishing
2375 E. Tropicana Avenue
Suite 8-305
Las Vegas, Nevada 89119 USA

Version 1.03, July 2024

eBook: 978-1-68500-070-7
Paperback (Amazon): 978-1-97463-320-3
Paperback (IngramSpark): 979-8-88878-864-6

THE SHADES OF LIGHT TEAM

**Shades of Light Team
Beta Editor / Readers**

Robin Heath
Trista Collins
Lori Owens
Nipa Jhaveri

JIT Beta Readers

Paul Westman
James Caplan
Joshua Ahles
Kimberly Boyer
Alex Wilson
Keith Verret
John Raisor
Kelly O'Donnell
Brent Bakken
Thomas Ogden
Ginger Sparkman

If we missed anyone, please let us know!

Editors

Diane Newton
Candy Crum

PROLOGUE

Larick reached the top of the hill before his fellow mystic, Volney, and therefore felt like the beauty of the view was his and his alone. They had traveled over land and sea to reach this spot, and as the wind whipped at Larick's heavy robes, casting them about like thrashing waves, he felt as one with nature.

Spread out before him was Roneland, the top portion of an island divided since the Age of Madness. Remnants of a city, old ruins of buildings that once reached into the heavens from the days of technology toppled and largely covered in vines and earth in spots, some completely overgrown so that they appeared to be new hills.

The ghosts howled, though Larick knew it to be simply the wind blowing through those old ruins, as he had heard those same ghosts many times before. He stood with the sea behind him, the green, rolling hills flowing in every direction, with the highlands just visible, rising up in the distance.

Heavy breathing came from his right, pulling him from the moment. He turned to see Volney, a shorter man with a shaved head like Larick's, but with piercing blue eyes. Though the man was less physically intimidating, when those eyes turned white the man was a force to be reckoned with.

"If only I could learn to simply levitate," Volney said between breaths, holding his chest, "this would be so much simpler."

"You know, brother," Larick replied with a taunting smile, "you could also spend more time on the physical."

"And lose time from my mental studies? Hardly."

For the first time, Volney looked up at Roneland and all exhaustion melted from his expression, replaced with awe.

"This is the place?" he asked. "Where are all the people?"

"My records indicate we'll not find them in, or even around, the cities. Here, from what I'm told, the people scattered, avoiding the cities and turmoil, holding their own in the mountains on the one hand, or creating great fortresses in the lowlands."

"There," Volney said, eyes glazing over for a moment as he mentally reached out, sensing life. He pointed to a cluster of trees on a far hill. "Not more than a couple dozen, though."

"The clans are like that here." Larick pulled out his parchment, checking his notes. "Yes, small groups, though we'll probably find some larger ones as well, and it seems they've come together in the lowlands."

"And magic?"

"Rudimentary at best, I'd imagine. No one was able to give me more than that, but since they've had no one to teach them until now, I can only assume it's a wild practice. Boys and girls discovering hints of magic, but unable to control it."

"Or even if they can control it, such powers may be unlike anything we've ever seen."

"Again, rudimentary at most."

Volney motioned to their right. The wind at the edge of a cliff was looking up at them, oddly enough. It shifted, then danced as it materialized further into the form of a small, translucent woman. She moved with the wind, circling them, and then came to a stop a foot from Larick's face, tilting her head to look at him.

"I see we're not alone," Larick said.

"Do you want me to...?"

"No, allow me." Larick put away his parchment and closed his eyes, focusing his inner eye, searching for the source of this spell. Oddly, he found only one presence nearby, that of a child. With a gentle soothing, he opened his eyes to see the wind spirit return to the air, flowing halfway down the hill. There, waiting, was a pair of wide, surprised eyes. A small girl, wearing nothing but brown rags.

Larick mentally projected himself forward, so that he appeared in front of her, though in fact he hadn't moved at all, and he said, "There's nothing to be afraid of, child. Not from us."

With a giggle, the young girl ran off, soon disappearing into a clump of trees below.

"Rudimentary?" Volney laughed. "I have a feeling we'll learn as much as we will teach, brother."

Larick nodded in agreement. He had to admit, he hadn't been expecting this.

They were in for one *hell* of an adventure.

CHAPTER ONE

Flames burst forth from the farmhouse, the same one Rhona's brother had entered just moments before. Alastar, ever the hero, had drawn his sword and gone charging in mere seconds before, leaving her to hide far away from trouble.

Clearly, that wasn't an option. Not when he could be in danger.

She worked her way around the farmhouse, searching for a way in. A scream sounded, then the grunt of a man, and she decided it wasn't time to be timid. She ran for the open doors Alastar had rushed through, in spite of the black smoke that billowed forth.

The sight froze her in her tracks—her brother in his white and gold armor, his white cloak smoldering at the edges, circling a man in the black and green plaid of Clan Buchan, the fire users.

A warlock.

She had studied the various clans and what magic they

used, at least to the extent that the paladins had been able to chronicle it in their war against the evils of magic.

Her first thought was to jump in and help her brother, but the warlock spun, hands pushing out, and a wall of flame came at Alastar that caused him to leap back and call upon the blessings of Saint Rodrick for protection.

Watching the shield of light that formed between her brother and the wall of flames, she knew this wasn't her fight. But when a figure caught her eye, a cowering woman in the corner, she knew she could at least help her. She darted through the smoke, staying low in a crouched run, and knelt beside the woman. Her eyes were barely open, her breathing short.

"Sera," Rhona said, recognizing the woman from days in the market, where she and her father sold goat's milk and cheese. "Sera, I need you to stay with me."

Sera moaned, and her eyes rolled toward Rhona, but she managed a nod.

"Good, I'm getting you out of here." Rhona placed Sera's arm over her shoulders, while wrapping her own arm around Sera's waist before heaving her up.

Her brother's battle cry startled her and immediately turned her focus to see that his sword had been knocked from his hands. He had reached the Warlock and was engaged in hand-to-hand combat. The two were exchanging blows without magic or blessings, but their circling and maneuvering put them closer to the burning walls and directly beneath a rafter that looked like it was about to collapse.

Rhona knew she needed to hurry, so she pulled Sera with her, pushing for the back door. The woman nearly collapsed, but Rhona grunted and pushed on, supporting nearly all of her weight. Sunlight met them as they emerged from the smoke and fire, and fresh air filled her lungs.

Then, she saw Sera's father, lying next to the tree line. She pulled Sera over to his side, then helped her to sit next to her father on the grass before turning to check his pulse. He was still alive, though unconscious.

Another shout came from inside and this time flames blew out from every window and the doorway, followed by a cry that was unmistakably Alastar.

Her own safety meant nothing if she didn't have him.

Throwing caution to the wind, she sprinted for the doorway. As the flames pulled back, she leaped in, dress pulled up to her face to block out the smoke.

Flames were all around her brother, pushing in on him and the circle of light that was protecting him but fading by the second.

Desperately looking around, Rhona spotted her brother's sword on the ground. She ran for it and heaved it up with both hands, but hadn't counted on it feeling so heavy. She had trained with it many times, but this time wasn't the same. Every muscle in her body strained as she tried to lift it, hoping to charge the warlock and impale him on its holy blade. It was hopeless, though, because even as she dragged it toward him, his eyes darted toward her.

A look of confusion crossed his face, fading to determination as he lifted a hand and the nearby flames moved toward her like the river after the breaking of a dam.

In that moment, nothing else mattered—only her life, and that of her brother. The sword fell from her hands, and they seemed to lift on their own, aimed at the man, and everything darkened. She wasn't sure what was happening, except that the flames pulled back, and the warlock collapsed to his knees, eyes turning black. A long scream came from his mouth as dark tendrils of mist or shadow, she wasn't sure what, wrapped around his limbs and throat.

And then he was falling, collapsing to the ground.

What followed was a blur. She would have sworn it was a dream, if everything in her wasn't tearing at her, pushing pain throughout her body. Her instinct pulled her to her brother, and he to her.

They fell into each other's arms, both on the edge of collapse.

"Wh—what happened?" he asked, eyes darting from her to the fallen warlock and back.

She stared at him, unable to answer. How could she, when she herself didn't know what had happened?

The flames roared and then seemed to be spinning around them. Could the warlock be up and doing this? She tried to turn, to fight again, and then collapsed.

When she came to, her eyes opened to reveal dusk had settled upon the land. She was lying on a cow-drawn cart, Sera at her side, her brother leading the cows. Staggering along behind them, bound and tied to the wagon, was the warlock.

Sera saw that she was awake and brushed the hair from Rhona's face with a gentle smile. "We made it, Rhona. Thanks to the bravery of your brother and the blessings of Saint Rodrick, we all made it."

Rhona groaned in pain, her body hurting like hell, so she let her eyes close and sleep take her again.

Yes, thanks to her brother… and whatever the hell had come over her. She must never let him know about it. She must never let anyone know.

Alastar had just finished wiping a smudge of dirt from his gold-rimmed, pure white armor when his sister, Rhona, entered. She gave him that look he always hated—a raised eyebrow, a gaze that dared him to look away from her green eyes, and a hint of a smile at her lips. It was the look she gave him whenever she was about to knock him back down to size and remind him of their humble beginnings.

"Let me stop you right there," he said, fastening his gold cloak over his shoulders and turning to the mirror. Damn, he looked good. Not in a conceited, sexy sort of way, but as a strong paladin who deserved every bit of honor the High Paladin, Sir Gildon, was about to bestow on him.

Making eye contact with Rhona, he attempted to match her confidence as he said, "I earned this."

"Oh, and I had nothing to do with it?"

"You were there when I needed you, aye. But I was the one who caught the warlock. I am the paladin here, don't forget."

"How could I ever?" Her brow furrowed into a glare that lasted only a moment. "I'm simply looking out for you." She stepped up beside him and reached a hand over to smooth out his cloak. "It's just… there've been too many times we thought he was preparing to send you on the holy quest."

"I have proven myself." Alastar turned, voice rising in his excitement. "Why shouldn't Sir Gildon send me on the next expedition?"

She shrugged. "He should, there's no doubt. But that doesn't mean he will. You don't notice the way he eyes me."

"The High Paladin? His holiness?" He waved her off, then approached the table at his bedside, where he had his sword and sheath laid out. "I won't hear it again." He strapped on the sheath, then hefted the sword and felt its balance. The jewels in its hilt made it seem gaudy to some, but the Order of Saint Rodrick believed swords above all else held a spiritual connection. They should be adorned, but it was more than that. When the Saint blessed their prayers in times of combat, these precious stones would glow as if they had a light of their own. Proof of the Saint's miracles.

"Brother…"

"He is the head of this order, the senior paladin in all of Roneland," Alastar said, sheathing his sword. "He does not covet my sister."

She nervously glanced around, as if the walls had ears, then wrapped an arm around herself as her free hand fidgeted with the blue cloth of her dress. It complimented her strawberry hair nicely, giving her a playful look that most paladins might not agree with, but simply reminded Alastar of the joys of their youth.

"Well, let's not keep them waiting then," Rhona said, heading for the door.

With a brush of his hair, he turned to follow her. They

would be toasting to him this evening, and he certainly couldn't be late in such a situation. It ate at him that the High Paladin hadn't seen fit to send him on the holy quests, but he would get his chance, he was certain of it.

Finding the Holy Sword of Saint Rodrick would give the paladins the power to fight off the invaders from the sea to the north, thereby earning their place at the King's right hand.

And if Alastar was the one to find it for his lord, he would be second to none in the Order of Saint Rodrick, except Sir Gildon, naturally.

He passed halls lined with armor and images of the Sword of Light. Its likeness was in these paintings and embroideries and elsewhere throughout the castle on shields and more. Its hilt was encrusted with the mystical green rock known as jade, giving its blade a distinctively green glow when blessed, a rarity, as other blades would always simply glow a whitish-gold, regardless of the stones they were adorned with.

This was all speculation, however, as the real one had gone missing over one-hundred years before, when Saint Rodrick led the attack on the creatures of Madness who populated Sair Talem, the large island to the west.

A pleasant aroma came from the main hall—the scent of roast pheasant cooked with thyme, apricots, and in white wine, if he had to guess. It made his mouth water. He could tell his sister must have noticed the scent as well, because she had stopped, one hand on the wall.

But as he approached, he realized that something must be wrong. His armor clanked as he darted to her side and reached up to touch her face.

"You're cold."

"It's…" She looked up at him with dark gray in her normally green irises, shadows under her eyes over pale skin. "I'm fine." The prayer was already on his lips as he reached for her, but she pulled back. "No, keep your energy." She smiled, and already the darkness seemed unnoticeable, the color returning to her cheeks.

"Your health means more than anything to me. Are you getting enough sleep?"

She nodded, but a distant look in her eyes made him wonder if she was holding something back.

They had never kept secrets from each other, at least, not that he knew of. Ever since their parents were killed in the magic wars and the Paladin order had agreed to take the two of them in, it had been so. He had promised to take care of her and to always be everything she needed in an older brother.

So now, too, he looked into her eyes and said, "If you need me to take you to your bed, all of this can wait."

"No, I'm feeling much better now." She put on her best smile and added, "Honestly."

A gnawing feeling in his gut told him to refuse to believe that. But she was his sister. If she said it was so, she was old enough to know the difference. She had reached her nineteenth birthday just two weeks prior, after all.

"Let's get in there and overindulge, shall we?" She took his arm and smiled up at him, waiting.

"I'm famished," he replied, and led the way, wondering the whole time if she was using him for support because she was still feeling weak.

The large, oak doors were wide open, so that the flickering torchlight cast a warm glow on the stone walkway as they approached. Inside, Alastar noted his brothers in arms at the head table, their ladies in waiting, men at arms, and servants occupying the rest of the room. It wasn't arranged like the King's great hall down south in Gulanri, but more like a church with a large tapestry at the front of the room that had on it the image of the glowing sword of Saint Rodrick. It framed Sir Gildon's seat nicely, situated at the top of the stairs, alone, with his own personal table for meals.

An approving glance found its way to Alastar as he entered, but just as quick, the High Paladin had returned to his meal, as if the rest of the world didn't exist.

"Come, I'll escort you to your table," Alastar said to his sister.

She pulled her arm free and shook her head. "That would make me appear weak. We can't have that."

He frowned, but nodded. "If you have any troubles…"

"You're halfway across the room, not off in the highlands or something. I'll be fine."

She patted his arm and walked off, leaving him to watch her go. He knew no other love like this. His last living relative, sharing the blood of the mother and father the two would never know.

He had his paladin brethren, but would otherwise feel lost without her.

But as she had said, this was his night. His opportunity to finally shine like so many had before him and, he hoped, have a chance to fulfill his holy duty. He wanted nothing more than to go on the quest, recover the Sword of Light, and earn the respect of Sir Gildon.

"There he is, the warlock hunter of the hour!" Sir Taland stood, the tallest of the paladins, with flowing blond hair. He motioned Alastar over to a seat on the bench at his side. Others nodded their respect as he sat, many of them having been in his spot before, but not all.

"Do tell—" the dark-skinned, gaunt paladin sitting across the table, Sir Bale, leaned forward, eyes glimmering in the torchlight "—what form of the dark arts did he manifest against you?"

Alastar relished the moment. He leaned back, letting the anticipation build as the others waited for his answer.

"Fire," he finally said, and motioned with his hand as if creating fire himself. "The barn was already aflame when we arrived, and when I stepped in to defend the lady Sera, he threw a wall of flame first, followed by an actual ball of fire."

"Odd how he hasn't used a lick of magic down there in the dungeons," Taland said. "The minute we capture them, nothing. Which makes me wonder…"

"He's one of them," Alastar said, affronted at the implied accusation, "you can see the singe marks on my other cloak, if you'd like."

"It's not that I don't trust your word, brother," Taland said. "It's that these bastards are all the same. They use magic against us and our countrymen when out there, but once they're surrounded by a bunch of paladins? Nothing."

"They know magic, sure enough," a rough voice said from behind, and Alastar twisted to see that Sir Gildon had been listening and actually joined in the conversation. "But they are evil, as all magic users are. Evil is like the darkness. How can it continue to exist when surrounded by such light as ourselves?"

The others nodded and murmured their agreement. It was known that magic users were evil. If they were wrong, why would the Saint give them blessings so? It was certainly a holy sign of their true beliefs.

Alastar couldn't help but notice a darkness cross his sister's expression as she turned back to look at the High Paladin. Was she offended at something he had done? While the High Paladin was pure and a true knight to look up to, Rhona often heard tales of him mistreating servants, and let them get to her.

Alastar brushed it off as not important for now, but made a mental note to ask about it later.

Sir Gildon's eyes turned to the nearest torch, where he lost himself in thought for a moment. For Alastar, this man was everything he wanted to be. Honorable, devoted and had a direct line of power to their Saint. All the man had to do was pray over water to make it holy, and run his hand over gem stones in their armor or weapons to bless it with the Saint's powers. There was none more deserving of the paladins' devotion in all the land, and none better suited to lead this war against the evils of magic.

As the flames flickered in his eyes, the High Paladin blinked, then rose to stand. The hall fell silent.

"My warriors of the Saint, my paladins, and our followers, today another blow has been dealt in the war against evil. A user of magic, a warlock, was reported to be within our territory, and justice was dealt swiftly. He sits in our dungeons as we speak, awaiting punishment. Who do we owe this to?"

The room turned their gaze to him intently, Alastar straightening up with anticipation.

"First and foremost," the high paladin continued, "the almighty Saint Rodrick. For all deeds are done through his favor. But we must not forget our own, our servants of the light, and today that honor goes to Sir Alastar Blackthorne!"

Cheers erupted from the paladin table, mugs clanking against wood and feet stomping.

The high paladin smiled down at him, the tapestry with its shining sword standing out strong in an almost halo effect. "Tomorrow, he joins the next group in the holy quest. Let it not be said that I forget those loyal to the cause. Let it not be said that practitioners of magic are allowed to roam freely. They will all be punished!"

More cheering rose throughout the great hall.

"But tonight, we celebrate!"

With that he lowered his head and said a prayer under his breath. He opened his eyes, still glimmering gold from the prayer, and then motioned to the great hall where, at once the torches went out, but a brilliant, gleaming light spread across the stone ceiling.

No matter how many times the men at arms and servants saw this small miracle, it awed them. Hell, Alastar's prayers were often answered, and yet, he still found these miracles inspiring.

Servants began to pour out of the side-doors with the platters of food Alastar had smelled on his way in. Everything from the roast pheasant to mounds of potatoes, fruits, alternate main dishes of blood pudding and sausages.

The men at arms were given jugs of ale and other spirits, though the paladins abstained, as was their holy duty. Men regaled each other with war stories, such as the time Sir Taland had stood up to a dozen clansmen by himself and bested their witch, a woman who had conjured a water spirit and attempted to drown him with her evil magic.

Alastar wasn't sure he believed such stories, but he went along with the laughter just like the men to his right. More than once, however, he found himself glancing over to his sister to make sure she wasn't feeling ill again. So far, no negative signs aside from the annoyed look she gave him the fourth time she caught him.

As they ate their dinner and laughter surrounded them, Alastar's friend, Stone, leaned over and held his knife like a sword. The man was built like a pile of stones, but that's not the only reason he got the name—one day they'd come across a wind mage who had attacked them without warning and, while the rest were clinging to the nearest tree for their lives, Stone had charged the man. He was lifted into the air by the winds, but not before managing to cleave the mage's head from his shoulders. That, they all had figured, proved the man had some massive stones between his legs. So it had stuck. Some of the ladies of the castle had tried to find out if the legend was true, but he stuck to his oaths, far as Alastar could tell anyway.

"You been training, Al?" Stone said. "You go out there on the holy quest at my side and don't know how to swing your blade, me and you got a problem."

"Last time we were on the sparring field, what happened?"

Stone grunted and jabbed his knife into the chicken

breast before him, but grinned. "Luck's what happened, and we both know it."

"Let me say this, Stone. The two of us go into battle, I'm not leaving your side for a minute. I promise I won't let the big bad remnant hurt you."

The others nearby laughed at that and Stone grinned. Alastar, for his part, didn't find the idea of remnant humorous at all. They were like men, but wild, crazed, and as far as the stories went, focused entirely on violence. They could not be reasoned with. They only wanted to wreak havoc.

But he grinned at Stone, and nodded. The two had become friends in the training yard, as Alastar and Taland were the only ones able to truly take him down, and Alastar had only done so twice. Anyone that could take down Stone soon became his friend, which meant he only had the two friends. Everyone else still had to earn their place with him.

"You really think the boy'll be going?" Taland said, lowering his voice with a sideways glance up to the High Paladin. "Come on, Alastar. So you took down one fire mage. You didn't kill him."

"Lady Death has her hands full after all the gifts you've given her," Alastar said, jokingly. But then he added, "And the mothers and widows left behind have enough names to curse without adding mine to the mix."

Taland sneered. "If I didn't know better, I'd say you were on their side."

"Because I don't want to see lives taken needlessly?"

"They are the enemy. Their lives don't matter."

The others had grown silent now, but Stone tore off a

chunk of bread with his teeth and, with a full mouth, said, "All lives matter."

Soon the talk had returned to laughter, ignoring the little confrontation. It wasn't until the meal had been cleaned away and dessert was before them that the first shouting came from outside.

"The hell?" Taland was the first to stand, reaching for his sword. "Men, to arms!"

His followers pushed back from their table and were quick to move to the doors, weapons at the ready in spite of their rosy cheeks and more than one alcohol-induced stumble.

Another shout came, followed by the distinct sounds of swords clashing and men fighting.

More men were moving to take up defensive positions now, but Alastar's first response was to reach his sister's side.

"Servants and ladies, to the back chambers!" Sir Gildon commanded, stepping down from his seat as he pressed his hands together. When he reached the bottom step, he closed his eyes. "By the blessing of the great Saint, let the light be one with you all."

As he spoke, streams of light fell down upon the paladins, causing them to stand a little straighter as they were filled with courage and to grip their swords a little tighter as they were filled with strength. Even the men at arms stopped wobbling, and their rosy cheeks returned to normal as the light healed their drunkenness.

For a moment, Alastar's new courage made him want to charge out into the hall and confront whatever had come for them, but he shook it off, remembering that his sister was still there. He would see her to safety first.

"Come with me," he said, hand on her arm as he pushed past the others and made for the back door.

"You're hurting me!" she said, and pulled free. For a moment, that darkness returned to her eyes, the same darkness he was certain he'd seen back at the fire. But then it was gone. She shook her head, blinked, and then turned back to him with a glare. "I can walk on my own."

He watched her stride off, then jogged to catch up. "We need to get you to your room!"

"Then let's get me there, so you can go off and be the big hero."

"We don't have time to bicker, this is a real attack!" He stepped forward to move in front of her, not sure what had come over her, but certain it had something to do with the darkness he'd seen in her eyes.

An arrow whistled through the air inches from his face, and he felt himself pulled back, barely out of its way.

A glance back showed him that Rhona had grabbed him.

"You're welcome," she said, and then motioned him on. "Go on then, kill the bad guys and protect me."

He let out an annoyed grunt, making a note to bring up the issue of her attitude later, then turned back to the entrance to a hidden passage not often used.

"This way will take us right by their target," she said. "What would be the point in that?"

"Well, if they're still attacking here, it means they haven't gotten to him yet." He pushed on the tapestry that concealed a secret lever, then nudged the passage door open—it was heavy, made of stone to match the other walls. "Plus, I mean to ensure they don't have him," he added.

"I thought this was about getting your sister to safety?"

"It is, but you have to wonder," he pushed past another door and paused, looking back at her. "They've never sent a full offensive like this in the past, so why now?"

In the darkness, the glow from his face lit up hers, and he could see the realization hit. "Something about this one's special."

"Must be, right? Special enough to be worth dying over."

He turned, and the two descended the steps into the dungeon.

Donnon waited in his cell of this old building that had clearly once been a church from the days of before. The so-called dungeon had an old, rotted cross hanging on the wall, a remnant of the old ways that none in these parts understood or knew the meaning of. There were rumored to be some who did across the water, in other parts of the world, but Donnon wondered if it was all a lie and if there were even people left alive there.

He'd never seen any proof of it, so why should he believe it? It was dark down here, as they hadn't wanted to leave fire that he could manipulate. The only light came from short windows at the top of the stone walls, just at earth level. Even if he could get up there, he wouldn't be able to fit through those windows.

Yet, he had to find a way of reaching Clan Renair.

He cursed himself for stopping to help the woman and the old man in their burning farm house, and cursed himself again for not burning the paladin and the sister to a crisp the moment he saw them.

It wasn't like he could be expected to know they would have magic, or at least, whatever it was the girl had used on him. He had been fighting the paladin, simply trying to scare him away and get enough room to run, when the sister had stepped forward and the shadows went crazy. If he had to say what it was, he'd say the darkness itself was brought to life, but he knew that wasn't possible. Or rather, he hoped it wasn't possible. He hoped that everything in him was wrong, and that his senses had been tricked.

That was it—she must be a mystic, he decided. He had heard of the people from the temple near the Arcadian valley, those who could control people's minds. Why not make him think that some scary new magic was being used?

Of course, the stories said mystics' eyes went white, not black as hers had. He shuddered at the thought and confusion.

A sound came from above, and he stood still, listening. Shouting, clanging of swords, and a feeling like energies sweeping over the castle—the feeling of magic.

If he was lucky, a nearby clan had seen the paladin capture him and had chosen now for their rescue. He hoped it wasn't the Lockmires, who would just as likely chop off his head as save it. No, more likely it was the one who he had left in search of, Estair of Clan Renair. They weren't far, he surmised. He would be saved and would have found his goal at the same time.

He hoped.

A paladin shouted above and a clanking sound followed. They were likely facing another slaughter, but this wasn't Donnon's problem. They had declared war on the clans, after all. So, whose fault was it when they found themselves at the sharp end of a sword? Not Donnon's; that was for sure.

Still, he felt no craving for blood, and no need to see the servants and others meet their maker. All he wanted was to find Estair and make it back north with her at his side.

"Who is it?" he shouted, rattling the bars to his cell. "I'm of Clan Buchan. Are you friend or foe?"

A figure appeared at the top of the stairs, casting a long shadow his way. If it was foe, Donnon could manipulate the flames and take him down. But what good would that do? He would still be stuck here, in this cell, mostly helpless.

"You there, I need help. I must find the Renairs!"

The figure paused a moment longer, then scurried off. Donnon cursed himself for not trying more, but then a sound came from the opposite side of the room. He spun and prepared, in case he needed to call on fire, but it was just a rat, pausing to stare at him with as much terror as he felt in this moment.

Then it was gone, disappearing through the cracks, while he was stuck there waiting to see what fate had in store for him.

CHAPTER TWO

R hona followed closely behind her brother, pulling her dress up over her ankles to avoid tripping as they descended the stairs. This was foolish, she knew, but she had to admit that her curiosity was piqued. On top of that, they had the warlock locked up, so what could go wrong?

The stairs led to the servants' hallways, many of whom were sticking their heads out in curiosity at the sound of fighting above.

"Return to your rooms," Alastar commanded, storming past.

Rhona did her best to keep up, but her dress made it hard to move swiftly, and more, the servants weren't listening to Alastar's command. Instead, they crowded into the hall with questions about what was happening, hindering their progress.

At the end of the hall, stairways led to the dungeon—a result of transforming this former basement from an old Church ruins into the dungeon.

Rhona turned and shouted, "We're under attack! Get to your rooms and lock up if you want to live!"

That got their attention, and soon the hallway was empty.

Alastar looked back at her and laughed. "Couldn't you have done that *before* we walked through them all?"

"Shut up."

They descended the stairs as an explosion of flames burst from the far end of the dungeons below, casting a yellow glow their way.

Alastar held a hand up for her to keep back, then crept forward and ducked down to look around. With a nod, he stepped forward and was gone from sight. Whatever awaited them couldn't be as bad as the terror of sitting here in this dark stairwell, heart thumping in anticipation.

She took the last couple of steps as one, nearly tripping over her dress, only to find Alastar crouching, sword held at the ready. Dungeon cells surrounded them, several with warlocks inside. A guard stood at the ready, club in hand. He wore boiled leather over his tunic, and was *certainly* no paladin. Another blast came their way, but it was from one of the stairwells that led down—the fight had yet to meet them.

The scream that followed sent a horrible chill up Rhona's spine, and she found she was hugging herself.

"What's the plan?" she asked.

Alastar clutched the sword, adjusting his grip and glancing at the cell that held the warlock he had captured. The warlock clutched the bars, eyes wide with excitement.

"Is all this for you?" he shouted.

The warlock gave him a wicked smile and said, "I damn well hope so."

"What do you know of the Sword of Light?"

"Enough to know it won't matter if we're all dead."

Alastar didn't like that answer, apparently, because he stomped over to the cell and kicked at the bars. "You pull on your flames, and I'll have your head."

He motioned to the guard. "Key, now. I'm taking him out the back way. They must not get their hands on this one."

The guard stared, dumbstruck.

"If they break in here, and by the sounds of it, they will at any minute," Alastar pointed out, "all that stands between them and this man is you. But if I take him to the paladin's quarters, we can pray to the Saint for our protection, and there won't be a chance of them leaving here with him."

"And me, sir?" the guard asked.

"Hide behind bars, pretend you're a prisoner. They won't touch you."

The guard contemplated this, then nodded and began fumbling with the keys to get the cell open.

Another blast sounded from the passage above, and Rhona shouted, "*Hurry!*"

Finally, she elbowed the guy aside, took the keys, and fitted them in the lock. They turned with a click, and the door opened, leaving her face to face with the dark warlock. A dull glow from Alastar's sword, left over from the High Paladin's blessing, was the only light. It cast an eerie glow on the warlock's face.

She gulped, anticipating flames to burst forth from his hands at any moment, but it never happened.

Instead, he shouted, "Down here!"

"You maggot," Alastar said, grabbing him by the hair and pulling him from the cell.

A burst of light filled the dungeon and a clatter sounded. They all turned to see a torch roll across the ground, still lit.

"Oh… shite," the warlock said, and then he tried to run, but Alastar's grip was too strong. "Get behind cover!"

A moment's hesitation nearly cost them their lives, but then Rhona ran, pulling at her brother, snapping him out of it. With the guard, they all ducked into the cell as a woman in thick robes, her face covered, appeared at the base of the stairs with arms raised. Flames erupted from the torch, like a thousand fiery serpents leaping for their prey. A great sizzle sounded as they hit the walls, which Rhona and the rest were hiding behind, and then the lady was in the dungeon.

"Come out, *maggot*," she said with a raspy, humored voice. "It's time to join the winning team."

Rhona glanced over at the warlock at that, and wasn't surprised to see confusion on his face. He didn't know this lady, and that was a sign of something, though she didn't know what, yet.

Then she noticed the glow of Alastar's sword, falling across the dungeon floor as the flames died out.

"There you are," the lady said, and a moment later she was standing before them, on the other side of the bars. Her teeth were pointed, and she wore white paint that seemed to make her face glow, and her eyes had a fiery spark to them.

She raised her hands, palms out, and the smile grew.

A thud behind her drew her attention long enough for Rhona to break free from her brother and push out on the bars, crashing them into the lady, and knocking her to the floor. The first out, she saw a man dressed in similar garb to the woman lying on the floor with arrows sticking out of him. A glow filled the stairs, then a shadow as another, similarly clad man appeared. He scrambled and shot back a flame of fire from the metal torch he held in one hand. He swung a sword with his other, but it hit on the stairwell wall and something appeared through his back—his opponent's sword, Rhona now saw.

The white-painted lady pushed herself up, turning on Rhona, but by then the attacker had pulled his sword from the dying sorcerer and turned on the witch. Rhona thought she recognized him as one of the paladins from upstairs, but his armor was covered in soot, and so was his face and matted hair.

He stepped forward, sword raised, and fell to one knee. His eyes rolled back in exhaustion, and the witch stepped forward, laughing.

Her laughter was cut off, however, as two more stairways filled with the clatter of armor, and a moment later, three more paladins rushed into the room.

"Come on!" Alastar said, and he pulled her and the warlock with him, making a break for the stairwell they had come down. With a grunt of uncertainty, the guard followed.

"The war is over!" the witch shouted, pulling flames to circle around her, separating her from the others.

"We've won!" another voice said, and suddenly a man with long, blond hair appeared at her side, his eyes flashing white as he turned to look at Rhona. Then the other paladins charged.

There wasn't time to wait and watch. Rhona led the way, running up the stairs with the others close behind. Men shouted their war cries as fires raged below. Rhona and the others were now running back through the servants' quarters, Alastar pulling at the warlock.

At a cross in the passages, they darted left, making their way toward the High Paladin and the armory, where the paladins were likely to have formed a defense.

They had barely exited into the great hall when a great blast of ice tore through the room, pelting them and tearing at their skin.

Alastar was fast, kicking over a table and pulling his sister down beside him. He prayed for protection from the Saint, but nothing happened.

The guard and warlock were huddled down next to them, and Alastar glanced over, confused, before returning to his prayer.

Rhona voiced his confusion. "Why are they attacking when they could hit you, too?" she asked the warlock.

He glared, but started when a piece of ice punctured the thick table. With a gulp, he said, "No clansman I've ever known could do that."

Alastar's eyes opened, and he turned to the warlock, grabbing him by the robes and pulling him close. "You're telling me they aren't with you?"

The warlock shook his head. "Someone wants you to think they are, but—"

With a vibration, the table exploded, and they fell back. Rhona thought for a moment that she was on fire as she felt her skin burning, but a quick check showed that wasn't the case. Three men stepped forward. They wore thick, black and purple robes, and their heads were shaven. The one in the center waved his hand and a circle of spiraling shards of ice appeared before him.

"Give her to us," he said.

Rhona glanced around at her brother and the other two men, confused. *Her?*

She was the only female in the room, but surely, they had to be referring to someone else. Maybe the fact that the warlock was wearing a kilt might have confused them, she thought.

"You're not welcome here," Alastar said, sword held in one hand, the other over his heart as he prepared for a prayer.

"This is no longer your home," the man said, and then thrust out so that the ice shards flew at Alastar.

Rhona was relieved to see the pointed arrows of ice evaporate as they hit the wall of light. The strange man smiled and let his hands fall to his side as the one to his right wrapped his hands around what appeared to be an imaginary ball. Flames emerged from nothing, forming a ball of fire. His eyes took on a malicious excitement, and he thrust his hands forward, shooting the fireball at Rhona.

She stared in dumbstruck horror as it came, and then felt a jolt as someone plowed into her, shoving her out of the way. When she realized what was happening, she saw the warlock standing just where she had been seconds before, hands up, pushing back against the force of the flames with all his might. Both men were pushing harder and harder, so that the ball of flame rolled in place, growing hotter with each second.

A laugh filled the room as the third man stepped forward. "Paladins and clansmen working together? Not for long, I think."

He held out a hand, and his eyes went blue. Air cracked around his fingertips just before streaks of lightning seared the walls and floor as it shot across the room. It was like the power was almost beyond the man's ability to control, but he was corralling it, working to convince it to do his bidding. Then, it was upon the warlock and Alastar, flinging them both across the room as sparks flew. The scent of burnt flesh filled the room.

A bang followed as the fireball finished its trajectory, exploding into the wall beyond them and setting a tapestry afire.

Rhona tried to push herself up, barely aware of the guard fleeing. Damn coward.

If she stood by and watched or fled, they would die. Something had happened out at the farmhouse, and as she watched the man with the power of ice step forward, she considered going to that place deep within herself again. Pulling on those powers.

She couldn't. Not in front of Alastar, who was even now pushing himself to his feet. His hair was frazzled, his armor singed and no longer pure with its white and gold.

This time, instead of shards of ice, the man reached out

his hands and the floor frosted over. Within moments, ice had engulfed Alastar's feet and was creeping upward.

He stared in horror, unable to move except to look to his sister and say, "Go, go, as fast as you can. RUN!"

Her intent was to run, but not away from him. She made a move to reach him and found her feet slip on the icy floor so that she landed with a *thud* on her back, her breath forced from her lungs.

She lay there, wheezing, as her brother tried to focus on praying for a blessing. He couldn't, though—with each word, he'd open his terror-filled eyes and look down to see more of his body covered in ice.

The man who had shot lightning at them was laughing as he stepped forward to stand beside the warlock, preparing his next move. Somewhere in the distance, Rhona could still hear fighting in the rest of the castle, and she wondered who was winning.

Would all paladins, the entire Order of Saint Rodrick, be under attack at this very moment in their various strongholds?

A shout came and more men and women entered the room in the heat of battle. Paladins fighting sorcerers, all in their dance of magic, swordplay, and prayer. And none of it was going to help Alastar or this warlock who had thrown himself into harm's way for Rhona.

She was their only hope.

With a gasp of air, she closed her eyes and let herself go, let the darkness within take over.

A crack sounded, and she was standing, though she didn't know how. The attacking trio turned to her, their smiles slowly fading. She heard one yell to grab her, to retreat with her, and that nothing else mattered.

But she wasn't about to let that happen.

Everything became clouded over, dark. Then, she felt it, the shadows in the room all converged on her and everyone had stopped fighting to stare in amazement and terror as the shadows engulfed her like a thick cloak, propelling her into the air.

Without warning or thought behind the action, the shadows attacked the trio of sorcerers, and she was one with them.

***

Alastar couldn't pull his eyes away from the horrible sight.

His sister was using magic. Possessed by some demon, she had conjured evil itself to work on her behalf. To save him.

She was in the air one moment, beside a sorcerer the next, clawing at his face with what appeared to be shadow claws. Blood splattered and, before he could react, she had been engulfed by shadow and was at his other side attacking one of the others while her shadow remained to deliver the next blow.

All that was holy within Alastar said to be done with her, to flee and never look back, or destroy her before the evil fully took hold. This was no longer his sister, a voice said in the back of his mind. This was evil incarnate.

Yet, when one of the sorcerers reached out a hand and caught her in a grip that sparked with electricity, causing her to writhe in pain, Alastar's heart broke.

And suddenly, the ice broke away, and he was free.

"Get your hands off my sister!" he shouted, and charged.

The sorcerer had barely turned his gaze when the sword connected with his arm, severing hand from wrist, and Rhona fell to the floor.

All the shadows converged on her and, with a spasm, she fell, unconscious.

The sorcerer was screaming as blood gushed from his arm while the one with the power of fire lay writhing in pain, and the third had stepped back, eyes wide as they fixed firmly on Rhona. He reached for her, even mumbled something, then collapsed to one knee and curled on the floor.

Everyone in the room was staring now, too, unable to move.

Two things were clear in that moment—the first was that Alastar's sister had used magic, meaning that she could no longer stay here or she would risk death. The second was that, if that was the case, Alastar wouldn't stay either.

He prayed for strength of will and body as he spun, sheathing his sword, and strode over to his sister's side.

The warlock was there, too, slowly recovering, but not too badly hurt.

"What's your move?" the warlock whispered, eyeing him intently.

"Escape," was the only word that came from Alastar's parched mouth.

The warlock nodded, eyes warily assessing the room. "Best hurry then."

Alastar lifted his sister in his arms without a response,

then made for the stairs leading back to the servants' quarters. The warlock followed him, which still made little sense in the clouded state of confusion he now found himself. All he could process was that he needed to take his sister far away from this place that hunted and persecuted magic users. He made it down the stairs before the commotion started up again from behind, and even saw the servants' entrance before the first sound of pursuit came. He could only imagine they had been even more stunned than he had been.

"She's evil," the voice of Sir Taland said from the base of the stairs. "You cannot let her live."

"I will," Alastar shouted as he kicked open the door to outside. "Anyone who tries to stop me will taste my steel and breathe their last breath."

He didn't even turn back to see the paladin's response, but stepped out into the night air, vaguely aware of the warlock still following close behind.

CHAPTER THREE

Alastar cursed his luck as he ran from the castle as best he could while cradling his sister in his arms. His armor clanked and his muscles ached, each breath bringing a new agony to his ribs.

He had abandoned the Order of Rodrick for a magic user. An evil, horrible, magic user… even if she was family. He was a traitor to his brothers in arms.

Everything and everyone he knew and loved was behind him now, and they would turn on him if he ever went back. Everyone, that is, but the one thing that mattered most in his life—his sister. There would be no more grand feasts, no more early morning sparring with his brothers in arms, and certainly no holy quests in hopes of earning the High Paladin's favor. He hadn't even been able to go on his first mission.

His sense of honor and duty and everything else ingrained into him in his training had been tossed aside.

Instead, he was now a fugitive, no better than the warlock running at his side.

At the tree line, Alastar paused to catch his breath, lowering Rhona to sit up to rest her back against the great spruce. She groaned, eyes moving under their closed eyelids, but she remained fast asleep.

The castle behind them was in flames. Though the foundation was built of stone and would last it out, wood had been easier to use in the rebuilding over the years since the end of the Age of Madness. Distant sounds of battle could still be heard from within, and occasionally blasts of red or blue lit up a window.

"Which clan?" Alastar demanded. "I need to know!"

The warlock shook his head. "We went over this. Those men and women in there? They aren't from any clan, not in Roneland, anyway. I would know."

"They weren't the Storm Raiders, that's for *damn* sure."

"Unless they've adopted a new look, but it's possible." The warlock shrugged.

Alastar considered this. The Storm Raiders had been attacking Roneland by ship from the north for years now, but often in small raids. Nothing like this. As far as he knew, they didn't have the power to call on ice and fire.

Only the mindless roamed the large island of Sair Talem to the west, and the king would never allow such madness in his lands to the south.

None of it made sense.

"Regardless of who they are," the warlock said, "you need to get her out of here. If they win, they'll come for her. But if the paladins win, so will they."

"I fail to see what the sorcerers would want with my sister."

"Really?" The warlock gestured to her. "After everything she just did, they'll label her a witch for sure. I've never seen magic like that, have you?"

Alastar shook his head. He had to admit that he had no idea what was happening with his sister. She had always been the normal one, amazed at the first time he had prayed for the Saint to bless his sword, and it had glowed ever so faintly. Although, now that he thought of it, there had been that time when they had first learned the news about their parents, something had been off then.

They had both lived in the south then, in the King's lands. It was different down there, closer to the old days, elders claimed. The days before the Age of Madness. People mostly lived civilized lives, going about their day at a factory or selling goods at the market.

Everything seemed so simple then, so safe. That only lasted until the witches and warlocks came, though, slipping past the northern defenses and wreaking havoc on village after village until the King's guard beat them out.

This unending war was all the lands in the north knew. It had seemed so simple—root out evil and defeat it. Evil meant anyone using magic.

Unfortunately, his dearest sister had just thrown all of that on its head.

He turned to see the warlock staring, one eyebrow raised.

"What?"

"I could take her," the warlock said. "If you want, I could take her to the clan, see if they'll accept her. You return to your paladin friends and keep your honor, say you killed her, and no one's the wiser."

Alastar took a step toward him, fist raised. "How dare

you? This is my sister we're talking about, not some pup to be handed off."

He held his hands up in defense. "I'm only offering solutions."

"There's only one solution here, and that's what I'm working to achieve."

"Which is?"

Alastar thought about this for a moment, realizing the warlock had a point. Where were they going?

"It doesn't matter, as long as we're together."

"Is that so?" the warlock laughed. "You'll just wander the countryside until you fall down dead? Is that it?"

"Me, dead?" Alastar shook his head. "Not until those sorcerers have paid for what they did here. I will avenge my brothers and reunite with those that made it out alive… after I find a safe spot for her."

The warlock considered this, then added, "Donnon."

"Excuse me?"

"That's my name. Since we'll be traveling together, I thought you should know."

Alaster frowned. This was a magic user standing before him, a warlock. They were at war with the paladins. But since Alastar wasn't sure where he stood with the paladins at the moment, seeing as he'd stormed out of there with not one, but two magic users in tow, this might be all the help he could get.

"Alastar," he said with a curt nod.

With a heavy groan, part of the palace collapsed, sending stones and stained glass flying.

That was the northeast side, where the High Paladin had his room. Where the main paladin defense would have been formed just outside of the armory. If it had fallen, he didn't want to even think about what could be happening in there right now.

"I swear on the Holy Saint and the Sword of Light, this will end with my sword through each one of their hearts," Alastar said, eyes locked on the crumbling building.

"That's all fine," Donnon said. "But right now, how about we get the hell out of here?"

A cloaked figure appeared at the base of the fortress, bald, and it seemed he was looking up at them. The sorcerer reached out a hand, there was a spark, and then he seemed to lose his balance, wavering with a hand to his head.

"He's exhausted himself," Donnon said, almost cheerful. "The little rat's arse has used too much of his power. Now's our chance! Go!"

Alastar didn't need to be told twice. He turned and lifted his sister in one quick movement, and then they were off again.

They ran through forests, crossed streams, and had crossed their second hill before Alastar's legs buckled, and he nearly collapsed.

"I... I can't do this." He cradled his sister, eyes closed tightly as he tried to pray for the Saint's blessing, but none came. "What's wrong with her?"

Donnon stood tall and proud, but a look of concern smoothed out his normal frown. "Like the sorcerer back there, she's worn herself out."

"My sister's nothing like any sorcerer!"

"Be that as it may, or may not, the fact remains that she

used magic, of a sort, and it drained her energy." He looked up at the paladin. "That's all I meant by it."

Alastar pulled back on his emotions, telling himself to calm down. Losing it out here, like this, wouldn't help anyone.

"How do we get her back?"

"You mean her energy?" Donnon's frown returned, and he shook his head. "That's not how it works, it's about rest. Recovery. There's never been another way to get one's spirit back, far as I can tell."

"Spirit?"

"That's what we call it, whatever it is that drives our ability to call on such power. You didn't notice that it often manifests itself in the form of an animal or some other spirit? A familiar some call it, pulling on one's spirit, others say."

"The dark arts." Alastar nodded. "Call them what you will, but anyone who uses magic is evil."

"Including your sister?"

"That's not... I mean..." Alastar's breaths came short and heavy, his nostrils flared.

He noticed his sister's eyes flickering and dismissed the comment with a wave, then knelt beside her.

"Great Saint, if ever there was a time to heed my call for healing, now would be the time." He placed his hands on his sister's head and closed his eyes. "Drive these evil forces from her body, heal her and let her never use magic again."

He waited... but nothing happened.

"If I may?" Donnon stepped up behind him and Alastar opened his eyes to look back.

"You know the healing arts?"

"I couldn't heal a lizard's tail, not even the kind that regrows." Donnon tucked his thumbs into his belt. "But I know a thing or two about magic and you're going about it all wrong."

Alastar took the warlock by the neck in one fluid motion that involved standing and darting over to slam him against a tree. The action sent sprinkles of water down on them as Alastar said, "Don't you dare lump me in with filth like yourself!"

"Like me and your sister, you mean." Donnon laughed, then coughed as Alastar squeezed. "All right, you've made your point. But..." With a quick thrust of his hands, Donnon had broken free and stepped away from Alastar. "If you'd try listening to me, she could be healed faster. At least enough to walk and escape those monsters back there."

Alastar's chest heaved as he considered this, but the man had a point. They needed to move, soon, and he wasn't going to be able to carry his sister the whole time.

The words came out forced, each stress of a syllable dripping with contempt as he managed to say, "What would you have me do?"

"Seeing as you're not smart enough to understand what's happening here, I'd say to start with clearing your mind. Forget about me, and focus on two things—her, and your belief that this magic, er, blessing, will happen."

"That's all? Belief in the power, but not in a higher being?" Alastar asked.

"You're distracted with this and doubting your faith, now that it shines a red light on you and your sister. So, just assuming this is magic or something else, like pulling energy from another dimension, say, wouldn't it make sense to you that, if you don't focus and believe, it can't happen."

"For the sake of idiotic hypotheticals, aye."

The warlock grinned. "Great. I accept it. Now, simply do it."

Alastar turned back to his sister and closed his eyes again.

"No need for that," Donnon said. "The whole prayer thing. If it's just closing your eyes to concentrate, sure."

"How about, since I still consider you the enemy and want to see you burn, I do it my way until I'm certain it won't work."

"Suit yourself, lowlander."

Alastar scoffed, but when he bowed his head, he secretly didn't close his eyes. In fact, he focused on the black and gold necklace around his sister's throat and imagined his energy flowing through those stones. He imagined energy coming down from all around him, entering her with great healing strength.

But nothing happened.

"A curse upon you!" Alastar said, standing and turning on the warlock. "Why am I listening to you, anyway? You, who I found attacking an innocent woman and her father!"

Donnon raised an eyebrow. "That what the 'ell you think I was doing?"

"What?" Alastar stared, dumbstruck. "You cast fire, that was fire. You attacked me as soon as I arrived!"

"I could've killed you."

"Not helping your case!" His eyes narrowed at the warlock.

"I have no case other than this—I was helping them, not hurting them."

Alastar frowned, confused. "That… doesn't make sense."

"Ask your sister when she wakes. See if what she saw was different from what you thought you saw, and then come to me with accusations."

"You were on paladin territory, why?"

Donnon looked away, his jaw set firm and a hardness coming over his eyes.

"Tell me!"

The warlock's fists clenched and he spun on Alastar, but then his eyes settled on the form of Rhona, and he sighed. "Healers?"

"What about them?"

"There's a clan not far from our own, as the crow flies, but to travel around paladin territory would take too long." His furrowed brow let up as his gaze became distant, lost in thought.

"Someone you know is hurt," Alastar said in realization. "All of this… they must be very important to you."

Donnon nodded, then snapped his head back toward the direction they had come. "It seems you and I are both in need of the healer, at least until you gain your 'faith' back, or whatever you want to call it."

"Clansmen would *never* help a paladin," Alastar spat.

"It's not you who needs the bloody help, is it?"

Alastar turned back to his sister. He breathed deep as he tried to pray for energy, but none came.

"Help me," he said, barely a whisper.

A quick breath from the clansman's nose gave Alastar the impression the man was about to laugh, but instead

Donnon knelt beside him, gave him a look that said he couldn't believe he was about to do this, and then heaved Rhona up and over his shoulders.

"Get the hell up," Donnon said as he started walking. "We take turns until we get there. I'd wager by sunrise at the latest."

Alastar pushed himself up and followed, wondering what he was getting himself into. As uncomfortable as the situation was, however, he was doing it for Rhona. The Holy Saint had abandoned him. His paladin brothers would hunt him down for betraying them, and it seemed the sorcerers who had attacked had a special interest in them.

But he and his sister would always be there for each other, no matter what. Nothing else mattered.

CHAPTER FOUR

Birds chirped, one making more of a whooping sound than a song, and a cool breeze touched Rhona's cheek gently. *Wake up*, it seemed to be saying, and so her eyes fluttered open.

The sky was gray with a touch of purple at its edges. Leaves drifted past as the wind picked up, and she was reminded of her father carrying her on a day long ago, by the small lake near their childhood home. She had tripped and scraped her knee and, even though it wasn't bad, her father had treated it like an emergency, even carrying her the whole way home and making her a cup of warm cider. She had laughed when he winked, showing that it was all a game.

Wait a minute… Someone did have their arms around her. A man with the very distinct smell of goats and campfire.

"Unhand me!" she shouted as she lashed out. The result was that she quickly found herself in open air, falling. The ground smacked her on the backside, and she let out a groan.

"What the hell did you drop her for?" Alastar said, darting over to her side and helping her up.

The other man was the warlock, she now saw, and he was wiping blood from his cheek, where her fingernails had connected.

"She attacked me!" he said. "Of course, I dropped the maniac!"

"Pardon me for being surprised when I wake up and find a strange man is carrying me," she said, pushing her brother off and, in spite of being wobbly on her feet, taking a step toward him. "What do you mean by it, putting your hands on me?"

"I…" He turned to Alastar with a look that said *deal with her.*

"You were part of this?" she asked, spinning on her brother. "For all you know, he could've been sneaking feels and—"

"Hold on right there." The warlock laughed. "With the number of women waiting for me to 'sneak feels' on them, I can assure you that was not about to happen here with you."

"I'm not good enough for you now?"

The warlock stared at her with his jaw hanging open, then shook off his confusion. "You're not a bad looking lass, aye, but—"

"You see!" She spun on her brother. "Lecherous!"

Alastar was just staring at both of them with wide eyes. Now that the attention was on him, he didn't know what to do with it. He held his hands up and nodded, then said,

"Everyone, calm down. Rhona, if we'd stayed back there after what you did, we'd be dead right now, I imagine. Or at least, you would be. Donnon here helped, because I couldn't carry you the whole way. Believe me, I tried for as long as my body would let me."

"But you could've just healed me," she argued. "I mean, you could have just prayed to Saint Rodrick and received his blessing, right?"

He shook his head. "I seem to be... distracted." He cast a sideways glance at Donnon, and Rhona had the feeling she was missing something.

A thought struck her and filled her heart with dread. She had hoped the images in her head were simply a dream —images of dark shadows and more. She knew the answer before she asked the question, and almost didn't want a response.

"Why...? You said I would likely be dead. Me specifically... Why?"

Donnon laughed. "Because you're with me and mine now, missy."

She glared at him, but the anger turned to fear as she looked at her brother. "Tell me it's not true."

He nodded, slowly, his eyes unable to meet hers.

"I didn't want you to see... any of you." She held her hand to her mouth to stem a flow of emotion she felt welling up. "It wasn't intentional; you have to believe me."

"If you hadn't acted, we might all be dead," Alastar admitted as he stepped forward and took her in an embrace. "You're my sister; that'll never change."

She lay her cheek on the hard armor of his shoulder,

then lifted the edge of his dirtied gold cloak to wipe at her moist eyes.

"We have to keep moving, though." He gave her a squeeze and then turned to look in the direction they were going. "Donnon, you said sunrise. I see no sign of a village or any life ahead."

"You wouldn't," he said with a cocky smile. "If we were so easy to find, this war your kind has waged on us wouldn't last very long, would it?"

"True. We would've wiped you out long ago."

"Wrong. You would've attacked more openly, sure, but that would've just pushed us to your level." Donnon scoffed. "You, wipe us out? Give me a damn break."

"Sir, there is a lady present." Alastar gestured to Rhona.

"Don't give me that cow shite," she said, to his surprise. "You think I'm so precious, well, guess what? I've sheltered you, not the other way around. You're a holy paladin, but guess what? *I'm not.*"

Alastar looked between the two, shook his head and started walking. "Both of you then, watch your mouths."

She watched him for a moment, then realized the warlock was smirking at her.

"Don't look at me like that," she commanded, and then walked off after her brother. Her head was aching, and if she had to be realistic with herself, she was only being a pain because she was scared. Her mother had always pointed out that this was a defense mechanism of hers, though at the time, Rhona had no idea what that meant. Now, she was catching on fast.

Donnon caught up to her and said, "I apologize."

"What for?"

"Well, simply whatever has angered you." He motioned to Alastar. "He *did* just abandon his paladin order to protect you, though. Not that it's any of my damn business."

"It really isn't." She kept walking, doing her best not to focus on the spinning sensation or her dry throat. "Since I was out… where are we going?"

"We were looking for a healer for you, but since you're up… I imagine your brother's still going along because he has nowhere else to go."

"If I just went back to Sir Gildon, explained what happened, maybe this would all be over."

He looked at her with a raised eyebrow. "You realize this Sir Gildon fellow might be dead, right? That and, even if he isn't, wasn't he one of the main persecutors of magic users?"

"Your point?"

"If you want to commit suicide, find a less painful way."

"I'm not following."

He shook his head. "You know exactly what I'm talking about, and the longer you deny your use of magic, the more annoying it's going to be to me. I don't like being annoyed."

She laughed. "How do you live with yourself?"

"Ha." He glared. "Point is, you used magic, but your brother and his entire order are convinced magic is evil. It might be on you to show them otherwise."

"Except that magic *is* evil."

"So then, are you."

She scrunched her nose at that. "No, I've heard of this

happening to people. Dark forces have their grip on me, aye, but we can beat them, cast them out."

"You have a lot to learn about this new world, lass."

"And a lot to teach you about shutting up, so I can enjoy this walk without you making my headache worse than it already is."

He reached into his rabbit-skin pouch that hung in front of his kilt, and pulled out some leaves. "Break those, breathe it in. It won't heal you like one of your brother's supposed blessings can, but it'll help."

She did so as her brother stopped ahead to look back.

"The Holy Saint blesses those in need, and at his own time." His eyes lit up like he dared the warlock to challenge him.

Donnon just shook his head and continued walking right past him. At the peak of a rolling hill, he stopped and pointed to the rocky cliffs in the distance, part of a ridge that carried on for some ways, out into the mist beyond.

"There," he said. "At the base of the cliffs is where they'll be."

A break in the clouds let in rays of sunshine, scattered across the ground between their location and their destination. They pushed on, crossing fields of tall, overgrown grass, pausing at a stream to take their fill of the crisp, clean water, and went on.

By the time they could see the thatched roof huts, the sun had crested the hills to the east and was starting to beat off the clouds and fog.

"What's our plan here?" Rhona asked as they approached, walking between Donnon and Alastar.

"The plan is to hope that they don't kill you," Donnon

replied, "while I seek out the healer I came for. We go our separate ways and hope to never see each other again."

Rhona looked at his weather-hardened features, the thick beard, and wavy black hair that fell in curly locks.

It wasn't that she would miss him. By the Saint, no. She had just met him, and he was brash, unrefined. But he knew her secret and had helped carry her to safety. There was something about the whole situation that made her sad to hear that this would be the end of it.

Or maybe it was that she had never actually known a clansman. She had to admit, she had always been curious and not just whether they wore anything under their kilts, as her brother would often joke. She couldn't give a damn about that—she was curious about them as a people.

"Is it true," she asked, "that not all members of a clan know magic?"

He shared a frown of confusion with Alastar, who shrugged.

"Aye. Only a few, in most clans anyway," Donnon replied. "I've heard rumors of clans formed entirely of magic users, but believe that to be in defense after attacks from the paladins, or leftovers from clans largely destroyed in the Magic Wars."

"The Magic Wars?" Alastar frowned.

"That's what we call it," Donnon explained. "You have another term for it?"

Alastar nodded and said, "The Holy War."

"Why am I not surprised? And now that your sister is involved and you're a fugitive, what side do you find yourself on in this so called Holy War?"

Alastar's face flushed red. "I'm still on the righteous side; we've just suffered a minor setback."

"Is that so?"

"It is. I mean to see that those sorcerers pay for what they did to my home and paladin brethren. But most of all, I mean to heal my sister."

"Heal?" she asked. "I have a disease now? Some ailment you must see stricken from my body?"

"Don't you agree?" he asked.

She stood there, head cocked to one side. "I have no idea. But I know this—I don't feel like something's wrong with me. I mean, I know I've been taught that magic is evil, and it scares the shite out of me..."

"Language," her brother reminded her again with a frown.

"Get over it," Donnon said with a laugh as he clapped Rhona on the shoulder. "If the woman wants to swear now that she's out of the stuffy confines of your castle, let her. To hell with them, I say."

"Thank you." She beamed and gave Alastar a *so there* look, then blushed as they kept walking. She wasn't sure what was coming over her, but something about being tired and realizing that she had done magic—not once, but twice—and used it to save them, gave her more confidence in each step and made her stand a little taller.

What if she didn't want to be "healed" of this? What if she wanted to see a bit more of what it was? She was certain that whatever she had done hadn't been evil, since it *had* helped people.

If something saved lives, how could it be bad?

Donnon nodded to the cliffs and then addressed Alastar. "What do you say about getting into something less paladin looking?"

Alastar bit his lip, looking down at his armor. "It's not like we have other clothes just lying around, right?"

"You could lose the cloak, maybe smother the armor with mud and pass for a regular knight? Maybe say you're from the south."

The thought of doing so came as a shock, judging by the look on Alastar's face.

"I could never," he said. "The cloak and armor are sacred."

"You'd rather they toss you to the depths of the lake and see if you float? Because I have a feeling you don't, even if your so-called Saint were to finally answer your prayers."

"Insult Saint Rodrick again, and we'll see how your magic does against my sword."

Donnon hesitated at that, then sighed. "Honestly, if you were them and a paladin just walked up, fully clad in armor with a sword at his waist, what would you do?"

"Point taken," Alastar said, then looked over at Rhona, debating.

"If you're wondering what I think," she said, "I recommend you do as the warlock says."

Donnon rolled his eyes at being called a warlock again, but since he didn't argue it, he must've realized doing so was pointless.

"And when I march back with the Sword of Light to present it to the High Paladin, you two would have me covered in mud? I will not!"

"The Sword of Light?" Rhona shook her head, trying to make sense of this. "How do you expect to find something no one before you has had any luck in finding?"

"With the help of him," Alastar said, nodding to Donnon.

"Me?" Donnon scoffed. "Self-absorbed and delusional, I see."

"The war against your kind hasn't been purely out of a desire to punish the wicked," Alastar said, lowering his voice. "We know your people have knowledge that can help us in the search for the lost sword."

"You've been hunting us down and what, torturing us for information on some mythical sword lost one-hundred years ago? That's sick."

"If we find it, nothing can stop us. Forget the clans and their warlocks and witches, I'm talking the Storm Raiders even. Then the lands will be united, with the Order of Rodrick at their head right alongside the King." Alastar's eyes shone with excitement. "Don't you see what good this could do? These lands were once united, I'm told. Long before the Age of Madness, there was one ruler, and we were prosperous. Now look at us. This doesn't need to go on, there can be an end to it… if you just tell us what you know."

Donnon shook his head. "First of all, a land co-ruled by the paladins sounds like my worst nightmare. Second… even if anyone had such information and wanted to share it, it wouldn't be me. You need to speak to our Laird, the chief of the clans. See if you can convince him such a world is for our best."

"It's not likely," Rhona chimed in.

"Not bloody likely at all."

Alastar ran a hand through his hair, eyes to the clouds above. "You two continue doubting, but I see no other way of keeping the Storm Raiders from our land. Whatever threat those sorcerers who attacked us last night pose, there might be much more room for paladins and the clans working together in the near future."

"Aye, there might be." Donnon pointed past them, through the trees to a figure moving toward them. "But right now, we have more immediate concerns. How about that mud, Alastar?"

Alastar nodded, biting his lip to hold back a curse, Rhona guessed, and then unhooked his cloak when a voice nearby said, "It's too late for that, holy paladin."

They all froze, but Rhona was the first to see the speaker. A woman in a nearby tree, bow pulled taut, arrow aimed right at Alastar. She wore clothes of blue and black, pulled tight and showing off her curves.

"Who are you?" Rhona demanded.

Before the lady could answer, Donnon said, "The Lady Estair of Clan Renair." He bowed his head and then added. "Clan Buchan sent me, we are in need of your assistance."

"And these two are?"

"Your prisoners, for all I care," he replied.

Alastar spun on him, hand on his sword, but an arrow came from the opposite direction, hitting the ground at his feet.

"The next will not miss," Lady Estair said and then nodded at the trees surrounding them. It was only then that Rhona noticed at least a dozen more men and women with arrows at the ready.

They had escaped the sorcerers, only to walk right into this. She would have to remember to thank her brother later.

CHAPTER FIVE

Alastar was furious. Not only had he been shot at, but now he saw one of those men aim an arrow at his sister.

Big mistake.

It was as if all of his worries from the last couple of hours were swept away by the river of his emotions by his need to protect. The prayer came to his lips even as he charged. A bright light engulfed him and his sister and shone from his sword even as he swung it to knock aside the arrow that came his way. He hadn't needed to swing though, as the arrow hit the edge of the light and flew around it as if swept aside by a mighty wind. It landed with a twang in a tree next to a newcomer's head.

The figure they had seen approaching stood there, at the outskirts of the whole situation, the arrow still shaking less than a foot from his eyes.

"Hold," he said, lifting a hand. The others immediately lowered their bows and arrows, but didn't take their eyes off of Alastar.

The man wore blue plaid, but black pants instead of a kilt. He wore a cap on his head at an angle and had gray in his thick beard. His hands were folded behind him in a very nonchalant manner, which told Alastar one thing—warlock.

"Name yourself!" Alastar demanded, sword held out with rippling waves of light moving along its blade.

"Curses, Alastar," Donnon hissed, head bowed. "You have the pleasure of addressing Laird Lokane."

"And I see you've met my master of war," Lokane said with a nod toward Lady Estair. "And you attacked, which makes me wonder why you're still alive."

"We didn't," Alastar protested. "They attacked us, and I defended."

"You are on our land," Estair argued. "The clansman is welcome. Paladins and their lovers are not."

"Sister," Rhona corrected her. "And… eww."

Ignoring that comment as nothing more than a sentiment he agreed with and not a slight against his looks or charm, Alastar felt compelled to educate this lady. "Paladins take no lovers, as it's against our holy order. We are above such physical temptations."

Estair gave him a doubtful look, then dropped down from the tree and stood there before him. "You can't be serious. You're not tempted in the least?" She reached up and loosened a cloth, allowing it to fall so that her shoulder was exposed, along with, just barely, the top of her breast.

Rhona gave him a nudge, and he realized he'd been staring.

"Yeah, not in the least," Estair said with a smile, and the others burst into laughter.

"Lady Estair," Lokane said. "That's not very… lady like."

"Neither would be screwing this paladin's brains out, but I'd be tempted to do it to prove a point right now." Alastar felt his blood flowing and had to adjust his armor in a most unholy way. The Lady noticed, and she winked. "Never mind, point proven."

Alastar felt his cheeks burning red, but refused to play by these uncivilized people's games.

"I'm a man, I never denied that," he said, standing tall. "It's the will not to act on urges that separates my kind from yours."

"Come now," a young woman still in one of the trees said. "Now, he's just daring you to bed him. Go on, get it over with. I'll find us all some good fruit and nuts to snack on while we enjoy the show."

Another round of laughter, cut off by Rhona shouting, "ENOUGH!" When everyone was looking at her, she stepped forward, out of the circle of light. "We come seeking sanctuary, not whatever the hell this is. The next woman who makes a joke at my virgin brother's expense—"

"They didn't know that part," Alastar interrupted. "But, thanks for throwing more kindling on the fire."

She rolled her eyes. "The point is, the next woman who wants to start something with my brother has to come through me first. And to be clear, I mean in a non-sexual, super violent way that will end up with you crying for your mommy. Got it?"

Donnon chuckled. "It's all in good fun, lass."

"Fun or no, it's over. You think I want to imagine my brother doing that stuff they said? No." She turned back to them. "So, here it is—we're, as of this moment, outcasts of the paladin Order of Rodrick. They would likely see me dead, as these two can attest. You can stand around and see if anyone following us shows up soon and then we can all fight them, or you can help us out, and we can all be long gone and avoid that situation altogether."

Alastar stared at his sister, impressed. He nodded and added, "What'll it be? Stand with us, or against us."

There was a long moment of silence, until Donnon took a step forward, to stand at their side. "We don't have all day here."

Alastar nodded to him, appreciating the act of solidarity. The others seemed to as well, because at a wave from Lokane, they all dropped from the trees and moved away quickly.

The Lady motioned them to follow, and said with a wink to Alastar, "Don't worry, I only bite when feeling frisky. You don't put out that vibe, so you're safe."

"And what kind of vibe *do* I put out?" the paladin asked.

"You know," she said and nodded to Donnon's direction. "You'd rather have the sausage than the pudding."

"Excuse me?"

"You'd rather climb a tree than explore a valley, am I right?"

He just looked at her, now remembering why he never got along well with clansmen and women. They weren't exactly civilized.

"What did I say back there?" Rhona asked the Lady. "Maybe I wasn't clear?"

"Sorry, sorry," Estair said, holding her hands up in mock surrender.

She walked on ahead to join Lokane, but Alastar saw them glancing back and talking about them, even as they started walking.

"Just, both of you keep your mouths shut and let me do the talking from now on," Donnon said as he walked past them to join the others ahead.

Alastar walked at Rhona's side, the two casting wary glances around as they made their way over rocky terrain and the odd patch of grass. Paladins and others from the lowlands weren't used to traveling through the woods, not without a group of warriors at their sides.

"What are we getting ourselves into?" Rhona asked.

Alastar assessed her, not sure how to answer that. "The better question is, what did you do?"

"I don't know what you mean."

"This is serious, Rhona. Did—I don't know—did one of the witches cast a spell on you? Maybe some sort of hex? Or a cursed item you picked up?"

She shook her head. "Not that I know of. It was just… I saw you in trouble back there at the farm, I thought Donnon was going to burn you alive, and suddenly I felt this dark part of myself opening up that had never opened before. Same again when I saw you in trouble in the fight."

A shudder went through Alastar as he thought about it. "When we're out of sight, I need to try a blessing again. Whatever's in you has to come out."

"Yes, of course." She walked in silence for a moment, then said, "But what if it's just part of who I am?"

"No part of you is evil, I know that. I've been with you through it all. I've seen the way you help an old man when he's trying to stand, but doesn't have the power, or when you spend your last pennies on food for hungry street children. No one else would do that, but you do."

"There shouldn't be children going hungry in the world."

"Exactly!" He motioned around at the green trees and rolling hills. "There isn't a person alive more caring than you. So, to presume that part of you could be evil… No, I think not. In fact, I'm certain of it."

"What then?" A puzzled look came over her. "Unless, maybe magic isn't so evil after all."

Alastar's hand went instinctively to his sword at such words, but he smiled at his sister and released it. "Careful there, sis, it sounds like you're saying the beliefs I've devoted my entire life to are wrong."

"Worshiping a man who fought off insane people?"

"Insane people intent on killing everyone alive, aye. If you could even call them people; they were monsters. Rodrick built the wall between us and the mainland. He was the one who helped rebuild in the early days. It's because of him we have this direct connection to the heavens, and because of him we're alive at all."

She gave him a pitying glance, and it hit him for the first time.

"You… you've never truly believed." He scrunched his eyes, trying to process this. "Maybe you witnessed the blessings, but I know you never bought into the Saint and talk of the Order. Your eyes lit up at the talk of magic, but not because you wanted it gone… because you secretly loved the idea of it."

He stared at her, waiting, and she couldn't deny it.

"All that time living under the roof of the Order of

Rodrick," he went on, "and it turns out you were just basically getting free room and board."

"I was watching over my big brother," she said, irritably.

"Watching over me?" He couldn't believe this. "You are my little sister. I'm supposed to be taking care of you. I can't even imagine what's going on in your head right now. Wait, did you… You didn't, I don't know, kill someone or do some sort of sacrifice?"

"Where the hell would you get an idea like that? No, I'm telling you, one minute I was there, worried about you, and the next, some sort of power was rising up within me. If I could explain it, I would. But I assure you, I did nothing bad and evil or whatever weird ideas you have going on in your brain right now."

A couple of the archers from their escort were looking their way now, and Alastar wanted to yell at them to mind their own business. Instead, he put both hands to his mouth, breathed out deep and then tried to clear his head.

"Let's look at this from another angle," Rhona said, caution heavy in her voice. "We were attacked, aye? And we have no idea who they were, but they showed up after I used this magic."

"They were able to sense it being used." Alastar wanted to hit himself for not realizing it sooner. "Of course. So, the key for us is to ensure that you don't use it again until we're ready for them."

"Right, though…"

"Though you haven't had complete control of it so far," he said, nodding. "Yeah, I considered that. Easy answer is we keep both of us out of trouble until that moment."

She laughed. "Keep you out of trouble? In the last twenty-four hours, that's been easier said than done."

"We hide out, help Donnon return to his clan, and then figure out where we can find the Sword of Light." She gave him a skeptical look, so he added, "We don't stand a chance against them otherwise."

A flicker of doubt crossed her face, but then she smiled and said, "Those bastards won't know what hit them."

"There's the sister I like to see," he said, nudging her with his elbow. "Who knows how many of our friends were killed by the sorcerers. Setting aside the war on magic or whatever we want to call it, I know one thing for sure—duty demands I see them answer for that sin. Honor compels me, and I wear her calling like a badge across my chest."

"Do you think Tina made it out?" Rhona asked.

"Tina…?"

"By the Saint, did you ever pay attention to my friends? Tina… she changed your sheets on weekends."

"You were friends with her?" he asked, then saw her look and changed it to, "You were friends with her, aye. I remember."

"Pig shite," she said with a laugh. "You never gave a damn for anything but your precious brothers in arms." They stood there for a moment in silence, and then she added, "All this talk of honor, wearing it like a badge across your chest." She gave him a skeptical look, then laughed. "You're corny as hell."

He joined in the laughter.

"I'm glad to see you two are in such good spirits,"

Donnon said, standing at the side of the path and waiting for them. "We're here."

Alastar was amazed at the village ahead of them. He had always imagined clansfolk to live in small huts in the mountains, to avoid the haunted hills like everyone else did. But right here, at the base of the cliffs and even rising up into the cliffs, were all of the old ruins he and everyone he knew had always been told to avoid. It was full of old ruins, mostly with dirt blown over them by the years with grass and trees growing on top. It made it so that you could barely tell there was an overturned vehicle with the words 'school bus' faintly showing.

Against the cliff, if you looked close enough there was what looked like an upside-down house. Because he had studied the earthquakes that had followed the collapse of civilization long before the Age of Madness, Alastar began to understand what had happened here.

Wind blew in heavy gusts, causing what sounded like distant howls of men and women lost to the old ways. Caves appeared scattered throughout in areas that would lead to underground buried cities.

He knew a woman once who had gone exploring down into those caves, but came out possessed, or so the High Paladin had said. Alastar had always wondered if her crazed ramblings about ancient technologies and an alien race were something she could have learned about down there, or whether they were simply the results of parts of her brain crumbling away.

She had been the closest he came to a romantic relationship. His curiosity had gotten the better of him, and he asked her about it. When she led him to the edge of one of these caves, he had peeked in and seen a picture of a man's face holding something that looked like a metallic weapon. The whole thing lay on its side amongst more broken glass than Alastar could ever imagine had existed, strange contraptions people said were called cars, though the word seemed foreign whenever they said it—like a made-up thing. How could they ever have made a piece of metal like that carry someone?

All of this old technology was down there, but rumors of skeletons and worse kept people away.

Everyone except poor Betty. When he had tried to turn back, she threw herself at him, crying, telling him he had to go down with her, to see the wonders she had seen, and then she tried to go down on him. It seemed like an odd time to do that, even if he hadn't had his paladin honor to keep him from allowing her. But she was crying and begging, undoing his pants as she knelt before him, and he was so confused he hadn't even been able to stop her until the warmth of her hand engulfed him.

His whole body had gone rigid, and, at that moment, he understood the feeling of sin. Trembling, he had pushed her hand away, told her that he was sorry, but he just couldn't, and turned and ran back to the castle.

Part of him still wondered what he would have found down there if he had gone with her, and what it would have felt like if he had never pushed her away. But he knew that was the evil, sinful side of him thinking.

He would never know, regardless. Within the year, the High Paladin had labeled her a witch and had her burnt at the stake. She was gone, and he had nearly been locked into it with her. If he had only gone farther that night, he, too, might have burned at the stake.

Staring at these caves now, he perhaps felt the ghostly presence stronger than the rest of them. He knew he wanted nothing to do with those caves.

Which was probably why his body went rigid with fear when he saw the others entering.

"You can't be serious," he said.

Lokane turned at the entrance, smiled, and said, "You have a problem with our home?"

Everything inside of Alastar wanted to turn away, to tell this man that he wouldn't take a single step into these haunted hills. But if they were willing to do so, then by the Saint, so would he.

He was a paladin, after all.

With a nod to his sister for encouragement, he followed Lokane in through the entrance.

CHAPTER SIX

Rhona wanted to laugh at the look on her brother's face as he entered the underground tunnel. If he only knew how many times she had been down in these types of places as a young teenager, he would lose it.

If everything her brother believed were true, could it be possible that Rhona's explorations into places such as these are what gave her this curse, or blessing, or whatever the ability to use magic was?

What else was she supposed to have done while he trained in warrior ethos and the path of the Saint, or practiced swordplay with his paladin brothers all day? She certainly wasn't going to sit around the castle, so she and a friend had gone out exploring. The treasures they had discovered were mind-blowing.

Old toys of the like they could have never imagined, some that even looked like the crazies had in the Age of Madness. A statue of a horse made entirely of metal. Food in cans unlike anything she had ever tried, from a world long lost... but too far gone to be edible. They couldn't bring it up to show anyone, unfortunately, because going into the underground was strictly forbidden. Even if you ignored the ghosts, these areas were known to have large drop-offs and to suffer the occasional collapse.

All of that being the case, she still wasn't prepared for this.

When they exited the dirt tunnel, its walls and ceiling propped up with large, wooden beams, they emerged into a great cavern.

Clearly, the clans had been busy.

Where buildings had toppled and fallen into ruins, the clans had carved out and repurposed, so that old metal and brick debris now served as walls to partially made underground keeps. The result was mostly uneven-grounded, square rooms with low ceilings, many of the rooms stashed with armor and weapons.

A clan woman looked up from where she had a torch on the wall and was manipulating fire to weld a spear-head onto the shaft, but Lokane stepped forward and closed the door between them.

He smiled but shook his head as he said, "You never saw this."

The others carried on, all moving into one large tunnel, except for two who went off into another adapted building to their right. They were at the base of a half-submerged building that looked like it had once risen up above the ground quite a ways, but now likely had crumbling old walls up there at best.

"And what *is* this, exactly?" she asked, glancing at her brother to ensure they were on the same page. He was staring around at the weapons in awe.

"You mean to launch an attack on the paladins?" Alastar asked.

Lokane shrugged. "A defensive strike is a better way to say it."

"That'll only serve to infuriate the High Paladin further, cause them to launch a full on offensive, to—"

"Correct me if I'm wrong, sir," Lokane interrupted, "but isn't it the case that we are already at war? I fail to see how us delivering a decisive blow will hurt us in any way. And besides, if reports are to be believed, your High Paladin may or may not still breathe. Am I wrong?"

Rhona could feel her brother's pain in his words as he explained that they didn't know, that they had fled the battle.

"A paladin who retreats when others are in danger?" Lokane shared a look with the others.

Donnon stepped forward. "This man is no coward. He chose to defend his sister… and me. He faced real sorcerers, and I don't mean magic users like us, I mean real, possibly evil, able to pull fire from nothing sorcerers."

Lokane froze at this, eyes locked on Donnon. Finally, he blinked, and turned to Rhona with a cocked head. "But what I'm not understanding is, first, how you escaped. Second, all of that just to run away with your sister? Couldn't you have stayed and fought?"

Alastar opened his mouth to respond, but Rhona held up her hand.

"I had exerted myself," she said, "so my brother chose to carry me to safety."

"And the so-called warlock?" Lokane asked with a nod to Donnon. "Why him?"

"At first we thought they were after him. It wasn't until later when they started talking about snatching me that we realized…" She trailed off, seeing in Alastar's eyes that she had perhaps said too much.

"Ah, but why would they be after a simple lady of the palace?" Lokane folded his arms, waiting.

Donnon frowned when the other two didn't answer. "Best to be honest here, lass. You're among magic users now after all, so no reason to be shy."

"She used magic?" Lokane turned to her with fascination in his eyes. "Well, is it true?"

She spun on Donnon. "You have no right!"

Donnon was about to protest, but Lokane put a hand on his shoulder and said, "We're all friends here."

Rhona frowned, looking at her brother who seemed as uneasy as her.

"I guess that's what it was… Magic, I mean." Her heart fluttered at the thought of using magic, and at verbalizing what she had done. It was like it could have been a dream before, but not anymore. Not now that she was admitting it. "Honestly, I don't know what came over me. It was like, one minute nothing was happening, and the next something came alive from within me, and it was struggling to get out. When I let it… poof."

"Poof?" Alastar said with a nervous laugh. "More like oh-my-god-what-the-hell-is-going-on-we're-all-going-to-die! But sure, 'poof' works, too."

She shrugged. "You get the idea."

"Not entirely," Lokane said, frowning. "Are we talking fire? Wind? Water? Did you see a spirit first?"

"No to all of the above."

"It was like the shadows themselves came alive," Donnon said. "Though, I suppose a spirit could've been there, just hiding in the shadows."

"Maybe, but maybe not," Lokane said. "You mentioned sorcerers able to pull magic out of thin air, correct? Though I've never seen it, I've heard tales of such magic. And if these sorcerers are doing the same, it's not inconceivable that they would be after you for a connected reason."

"Wait." It was Alastar's turn to look confused. "I thought all magic came from nowhere, like it just appeared. That's... wrong?"

"It would seem that sharing our secrets with the enemy wouldn't be the prudent thing to do here," Lokane said, pondering, "But since your sister is being honest with us, I suppose a little honesty won't hurt from our side either. That, and if I judge the situation correctly, you're basically stuck here with us until we can all come up with a strategy for how to deal with these sorcerers."

He nodded to Donnon, who stepped back and raised his hands. Nothing happened.

"See," Lokane said. "Donnon is a fire user, but he can't just *make* fire. When a man or woman learns they are a fire user, it is only after a fire spirit has visited them when there is a fire nearby. One might be using a torch when a spirit dances out, looking like a flame, and presents said person with their powers. Or maybe while preparing a hot stew, or whenever a fire is around. Likewise, with water, the user would have generally been by a lake or river."

"Then, to call on the powers," Donnon added as he approached one of the torches on the walls, and picked it up, "you simply have to be close enough to maneuver it, depending on your power with the spell."

With that, he lifted the torch and held out his other hand. His eyes went black, and the flames shot out from the torch, encircling him like a whip before shooting up and coming to form a ball of fire, circling in the air about an inch from his free hand.

He winked at Rhona, and then let the flames return to the fire of the torch.

Rhona's heart was beating out of her chest, and her mind overflowing with questions.

"And water… it's the same?"

Donnon nodded. "But not the same people. Clans who live by the water often discover water mages among them. Fire mages are born among the mountain clans, more or less."

"Come, we mustn't keep the council waiting," Lokane said, motioning them onward. "We'll have plenty more time to talk after breakfast is served."

Rhona couldn't help the small whimper of excitement that escaped her lips at the thought of food and drink.

"Don't worry, we'll take good care of you," Donnon said, stepping up beside her and offering her a hand so that she could step down a ledge that led to the path below.

She was about to take it, when Alastar stepped between the two of them, grabbed her by the waist, and lifted her down.

"I could've done that myself," she said, glaring.

"Then why would you be reaching for his hand?" He turned on Donnon. "And you, thanks for the hospitality, but you'd best keep your hands to yourself."

He stormed on ahead, leaving Donnon to grin like a schoolboy at Rhona. She had to admit, there was something charming about that grin. Instead of following her brother, or putting up with his being overly protective, she took Donnon's arm and allowed him to escort her on.

"I was feeling light-headed," she explained when Alastar glanced back and frowned. He was about to move to help her, when she said, "Just keep walking. I'm a grown woman."

"Barely," he muttered, but didn't say anything more on the matter.

"While I'm all for being used to annoy older brothers," Donnon whispered, leaning in to her, "I must warn you, I have a sensitive heart."

She laughed. "We can all tell, you big softie."

He pulled her closer. She thought about stepping away. After all, she barely knew this man. But after learning that not only had he carried her some of the way, helping her brother and her to escape, but that he was now entrusting them with this hideout and the secrets of his people's magic, she felt a closeness she had never felt this quickly with anyone before.

They descended into a cave where a woman fire mage bowed at their entrance, and then spread her arms out so that fire spread from two torches to run along the ground. The flames hit a central location and then burst outward, spreading along the walls so that there was one large circle of controlled fire lighting up the entire cavern.

Lady Estair had set up a table where several others were bringing out plates of food. Past that, several other passages broke off, looking like they led up. Some rooms down here formed out of more ruins, sheets of metal from those abandoned with "bus" written on the side, and all sorts of old knick-knacks piled up on the far side.

"What is this place?" Rhona asked.

"A collector's dream," Donnon said, nodding at Lokane. "That specific collector, actually. He loves this stuff. Says it connects us to our ancestors and even believes it might have some sort of old magic to it. Me? I say it's junk. Cool junk, but junk."

"It's… amazing."

"You see this stuff, you'd think his collection's complete, right?" Donnon laughed. "Not remotely. He has these tunnels set up for transportation, getting around without the paladins knowing, but really, I think it's his excuse to excavate, to see what he can learn about them—the people from before the Age of Madness."

"Have you learned anything, I don't know, of value?"

"They had many oddities, that's for sure. But you look at some of this stuff, like there." He pointed to a corner where a cylindrical metal object sat, with a painting of a woman on its side, twice the size of a real one. "They were artistic, technologically advanced to a level we'll never understand, and yet… not a single sign of them knowing magic that we can find."

"But I can't imagine what that would look like anyway."

He nodded. "True enough. Could there even have really been a world with all of this, but without the ability to do what we do?"

The idea of being lumped into the group of people who can use magic scared her and a lump caught in her throat.

"Why are you all telling us all this? Aren't you afraid we'll return and tell the others?"

He looked at her with trusting, caring eyes. "You'll never fit in with their kind again. I'm sorry to say it, but it's true. You're done there. The paladin, too, I imagine."

"That's quite enough," Alastar said. He stood at the table, holding out a chair for Rhona.

She smiled and said, "Excuse me," before joining her brother. She made sure to give him a very annoyed glare before taking her seat.

"At last," Estair said, her eyes lingering on Rhona and Alastar, "it seems we're ready to unite Roneland."

Alastar had just taken a sip from his mug, but nearly spat it out. "Excuse me?"

"The Lady speaks about an old legend here," Lokane leaned forward and offered him a plate of turnips and greens, "told of a time when the paladins would come to realize that their magic is not so different from our own."

"I'm sorry," Alastar said, eyeing the plate of food and finally accepting. He scooped some onto this plate and handed it to Rhona. "But what makes you think this would ever happen?"

"It's not about thinking. It's about hoping."

Estair nodded. "It's about surviving, if we're being truthful here. The Storm Raiders grow in force, so I'm told, and there are other threats. Your castle wasn't the first to be taken down by a small army of sorcerers. In fact, we learned of them a week ago when a man came here in tatters, shouting about death and destruction. Two clans united to form a squad of fire mages and ice mages to stand against them… but were destroyed like a dry leaf, crumpled and blown to the wind."

The others around the table shook their heads, each of their eyes holding the terror that Rhona felt coursing through her chest. In spite of her hunger and exhaustion, and the buttery smell of roasted potatoes that had been so enticing moments before, she now seemed to have lost her appetite.

"How can we hope to stand against them?" she found herself saying.

The answer came in the form of all eyes on her, and then her brother's mouth opened slowly before he said, "They mean for your powers to lead the defense." He stood, his seat flying backward. "That's why he brought us here, once he saw." He spun on Donnon. "You led us here knowing this?"

He shook his head. "I already told you, I came for the healer."

Estair narrowed her eyes at this, then said, "Ah, I received the message. You must be Donnon, then?"

Giving her a slight nod, he said, "We thought the message might not be enough to convince you."

"True, it might not have, and in fact, I'm forced to wonder why you wouldn't return to your own clan with this paladin, if you needed a healer."

His expression became grim at that. "The thought had crossed my mind, but these two needed shelter, and rest."

"So you put their needs ahead of your own." She nodded, pleased. "Here's the situation we find ourselves in. Donnon is in need of a healer, Rhona in need of a teacher—"

"I am?" Rhona asked.

"You are, or you may never fully understand the depth of your powers."

"I don't understand something," Alastar said, eyes focused on Estair. "You are apparently fire mages, or those of you who wield magic. In what way are you a healer, too, then?"

Her smile was pleasant, but with a deep sorrow in her eyes. "They asked that of my parents, too, before they took me from them as a young child. They asked if I was praying, if I was somehow trained in the paladin arts, maybe a secret training on the side. The answer to all of those questions was no, which is why I know your prayers are magic and nothing more. I know, because we have the same powers, Alastar. You and I are not as different as you want to believe."

He blinked hard, reached for his chair to sit, but ended up sitting in the open air where his seat had been before it fell backwards. When he hit the ground with a clang, he was barely able to stand again, and Rhona stood to help him to his feet, then righted his chair for him.

When he was seated, he took a long drink of water from his cup, then stared at Estair and said, "Show me."

She smiled, and then her eyes glowed gold, and the room darkened, just before brightening beyond belief. It was like daylight, and many had to shield their eyes as they adjusted.

With a wave of her hands, Estair let the light fade into a shield around her, much like the ones Alastar made, and then sent the light across the table to bathe Rhona and Alsatar in a tingling warmth.

The fright vanished along with the pains in Rhona's stomach, and the food suddenly looked appealing again.

"You see," Estair said. "Not a moment's prayer. You damn paladins think you're so much better than us, think you're holy. But our magic comes from the same place—and no amount of 'pure living' changes the fact that you're as human as the rest of us."

Alastar stared at her, eyes twitching, and then he stood again, turned to Rhona and said, "We're done here," before storming away from the table and back the way they came.

"I'll… talk to him," Rhona said as she leaped up from her chair. She darted over and caught up with him at the tunnel entrance. "Alastar, wait!"

He spun, but where she expected to see fury, there was sorrow in his glistening eyes.

"Wh—what do we do?" she asked.

He reached out to lean against the dirt wall for support, his posture bent as if the weight of the world was on his shoulders. "It's some kind of cheap trick. It must be. Rodrick sent that witch to test my faith. They can't expect me to forsake everything I've ever believed in, simply because some witch can replicate what the Saint has granted me."

"Then don't. Don't abandon faith, if that's what drives you. Is there a Saint Rodrick out there, looking over us in spirit or something? Hell, I don't know. But what I do know is that they make a lot of sense. If this army of sorcerers is moving through the land, and somehow, they can track where I am, that'll be tough for us to handle on our own. But if we find ourselves a team, if we go after the

Sword of the Light and find it, we might just be unstoppable."

"The power of light and the power of dark," he said with a laugh. "The pair we would make."

"Brother and sister, ridding the world of evil."

He frowned. "Assuming evil now means something entirely different from what we have always been raised to believe."

"It's an assumption we'll have to make. That, or burn me at the stake right now. Either way, this power is a part of me. I feel it too strongly to believe anything else."

He nodded and then took her in an embrace. "Tell them we're in. We'll help them, but… I see you with that Donnon guy again, I'll have to say my piece."

"How about instead, we're in, and I'll do whatever the hell I want with whomever the hell I want?"

Although he rolled his eyes, he nodded, and they turned back to the table to see the others watching them.

"We're in agreement then?" Estair called over.

Rhona nodded. "Just tell us where to sign, and it's on." They all looked at her like she was an idiot. "Oh, just… yeah, we're on board."

With a cheer, they welcomed her and Alastar back to the table, and made sure they were eating well this time. When the first bite of lamb stew filled her mouth with warmth and the taste of shallots and carrots, she closed her eyes and had to keep herself from moaning. She opened her eyes to see Donnon staring with a smile at the corner of his mouth, so she turned away, blushing.

"Remember," Alastar said, playfully. "Stay away from him."

She playfully kicked him, gently though so as not to hurt her toes on his armor. "You remember, stay the hell out of my business."

He laughed and then took a bite of his lamb, not even caring to wipe the grease from his chin, he was so lost in the moment of ecstasy.

From the sounds of what they were about to get themselves into, there wouldn't be much opportunity for rest and relaxation. They had better enjoy it while they had the chance, Rhona thought to herself as she took another mouthful of her stew.

CHAPTER SEVEN

Alastar knelt at the side of the bed they had given him, if you could call it that, in what was to be his sleeping quarters. This particular room looked like it had once been a half of a living room, with the stones that had made up a fireplace that was now caved in. The 'bed' was just several cloths thrown down on the floor.

He had found a corner to stash his armor and recoiled at the putrid stench that wafted up from his armpits, now that the armor was off. A bath would have been perfect after the feast at the castle, in preparation for his holy quest. Instead, those damned sorcerers had come along and messed everything up. He'd have to remember to bathe in the morning, if there was any sort of bathing facility here. They had drinking water, so if nothing else, that would have to do.

"Holy Saint," he said, hands clasped and eyes closed, "grant me virtue, honor, and devotion. See me through these hard times so that I may see you shine." He felt his head rolling as he nodded off, nearly losing the prayer to sleep. He wanted a lot of things at the moment—peace of mind, his sister to have never used magic in the first place, and to fulfill his honor and see that those who attacked the paladins should meet his blade.

But right about now, sleep pulled at his desires above all else.

His body would have likely cracked and ached as he lay down, if not for the healing spell the Lady Estair had put over him.

He rolled over on the cloths, trying to get comfortable, when he froze at the sight of a shadow falling across his room. In a moment, he was sitting up with his hand on the hilt of his sword.

"Can a man never rest?"

"A man could," came a woman's voice. "But then he would miss out on so much of life."

"Better to miss out and live, than to die from exhaustion."

"A man should let a woman care for his needs." She leaned against the doorway and, once again, the neckline of her dress fell to reveal more skin than he was comfortable being around.

"Even if I were at a point where I could be willing to betray my vows, I promise you, I haven't the energy."

"Don't worry, I'm only testing your resolve." She adjusted her clothes to cover the bare flesh and entered, leaning against the wall so that she could look down on him. "Thing is, I need to make sure you're loyal once you put your heart to something."

"Loyalty is my strong suit." He tilted his head,

wondering where she could be going with this. "But my loyalty still stands behind my faith."

"And yet, you abandoned your castle to see your sister, a magic user, to safety. You were getting her away from there as much as you were getting her away from the sorcerers, am I wrong?"

He turned his gaze to the earth at his feet, as dark as it was. The only light came from one of the torches out in the hallway, which was at this moment casting deep shadows across the room.

"It's only ever been me and her," he said. "I'd burn the world to the ground if it meant saving her."

"We start training tomorrow, after you have slept. I mean to show you that everything you've thought about life with those paladins is wrong."

He turned to look at her, unable to ignore the way the light highlighted her curves. With a simple nod, he lay back and closed his eyes.

"Guess I better get on with my sleep then," he said, and could barely hear her saying something in response as sleep overcame him at last.

Rhona only slept four or five hours, but when she woke, she felt completely rested. She returned to the dining area, realizing she hadn't eaten nearly enough the night before, and was pleased to see an array of freshly roasted vegetables and several loaves of bread.

No one else was around, so she helped herself,

wondering if her brother was still sleeping, but not knowing where they had put him for the night.

This was so strange, being in the hideout of the same people she had called enemy just the day before.

She was one of them, in more ways than she was happy to admit.

"At last," Estair said, emerging as she wrapped herself in a new outfit. Unlike the blue and black she had worn the night before, this one was violet with a hem of gold. "I trust you are ready?"

"Ready for...?"

"Ah, you must not have spoken with your brother yet then. We must ensure you understand your powers before we're ready to leave this place, when the time comes."

"So you mean to come with us?"

Estair leaned against the table and scratched at the wood with her fingernail, furrowing her brow. "Honestly, I'd prefer not to. But I have a feeling you're going to need our help."

"You haven't seen what I'm capable of," Rhona replied.

"Show me then."

With a frown, Rhona stood and concentrated.

Nothing happened.

She held up a finger, closed her eyes, and focused on everything within her, the good and bad energy, all of it floating up and out, around her head. But when she opened her eyes, again there was nothing.

"It's all very intimidating," Estair said with a smirk. "Thing is, staring at your pretty face will only distract them long enough for your brother to take down one, maybe two. But what if there are three attackers?"

"I get your point."

"Good, then you'll know why you have to come with me." She hopped down and started walking.

"What, now?"

"Your brother's still asleep, and you're not. Sounds like the perfect time."

Rhona couldn't argue, so she stood and followed the lady out of the dining area and into a tunnel that led upwards. Soon, a bright light shone that made her pull back, and after a moment of her eyes adjusting, she realized it was the sun.

"Outside?"

"You'll see."

They emerged into what looked like a large sink-hole. The edges above were guarded by trees, so that the sun only made its way in when directly above, as it was now.

"We train here, more often than not," Estair said, gesturing around to the torches placed around and a small pool of water on one side. "It's not likely anyone will find this location, as it's well hidden, and looks like a sink hole if they do find it. Too dangerous to be worth exploring."

She turned to Rhona and smiled. "First, any questions?"

"Probably more than you could count. But aye, how the hell do you expect to teach me magic when you don't even understand what my magic is?"

"Actually, I was hoping our guests could take a crack at that."

"Guests?" Rhona frowned, looking around, but seeing no one.

"They should be..." Estair held up her hand so a light shone, and then she pointed. "There!"

Two shadows had appeared on the ground in the shape of robed men. One moment there was nothing there but the shadows, the next, two men were standing there, smiling.

"Well, we couldn't just hang around all morning in plain sight," the taller of the two said. They both had shaved heads and wore thick, gray robes.

"I told you, no one comes out this way," Estair replied. "And if they did, they wouldn't come down here." She gave Rhona a *men, ugh* glance and then said, "Allow me to introduce Larick and Volney, two mystics from the Arcadian Valley.

Rhona had heard of the valley before, and that piqued her curiosity. "Mystics?"

"Practitioners of mental magic," Larick said with a friendly smile. "We've come here to educate, and see who we might be interested in bringing back with us to train further."

"I've never heard of mental magic," she admitted. "So you, what? Move stuff with your minds?"

Volney shook his head. "No, though, we could make you think we were. In simple terms, it's more about altering thoughts, creating the idea that we're doing something."

"I assure you, I don't ever need something dumbed down for me."

Larick laughed. "No disrespect meant, I'm sure."

"These two have been helping us to understand our own powers," Estair said. "Though, I have to say, I don't agree with everything they preach."

"What the Lady is referring to," Volney said, stepping

forward and looking over Rhona as if he was reading a book, "is that, we in the Arcadian Valley understand magic to be something within all of us, you just have to know how to access it. It's not that some are born with it while others aren't. It's that some learn how to access it, while others live their entire lives in ignorance."

"Basically, what he's saying," Larick cut in, "is that the concepts you all have come to understand as spirits, or familiars, and magic... it's all something created here, a way of understanding magic because of your cultural heritage, your past beliefs and mythology."

Rhona chuckled. "My brother wouldn't like to hear that."

"Many of our fire mages wouldn't accept it either," Estair said. "I'm still not sure I even do, but I'm willing to listen."

"It's a simple matter of discovering the magic, and finding ways to harness it." Larick frowned at Rhona, and for a moment his eyes covered over in a film of milky white, but then he paused. "Do you mind?"

She wasn't sure what he meant, so she shrugged and said, "No...?"

Again, his eyes went white, and this time, she felt a tingling in her head. He let out a yelp and stumbled back, and when his eyes returned to normal, he looked at her with confusion and awe.

"What is it, brother?" Volney asked.

"She... she is capable of something entirely different. Unlike anything we've ever seen before."

Rhona frowned. "I didn't come here to be analyzed."

"Please," Estair said as she placed a hand on Rhona's

shoulder. "I was hoping you could tell us what sort of magic she has, maybe help her understand it, learn how to harness it."

Larick looked dubious, but cocked his head to one side, thinking. "As far as I can tell, this appears to be physical magic, but of a different sort. It's possible that the Founder would be able to do similar magic, though I've never sensed this in him. It's…. dark."

"The Founder?" Rhona asked.

"It's a long story," Volney said.

Unlike Larick's cautious gaze, Volney stepped forward, excitement shining. "I don't suppose you could show us?"

"Show me yours, and I'll show you mine." She didn't even try to hide the irritation in her voice.

"Excuse me?"

She glared, unsure what to say next. After everything she had been through in the last twenty-four hours, the last thing she wanted was to be tested and probed. Whatever magic had taken hold of her or she had used, she didn't understand it in the least and had never wanted it to begin with. So, the idea of these guys standing there and assessing her, asking her effectively to put on a show, really pissed her off.

"We already tried that at any rate," Estair said, sensing Rhona's annoyance. "Perhaps it's best if you simply tell her what you know that you think could be applicable here, and then we can see if there's a way to draw out the powers to get a good look."

Volney nodded and began to explain that, in the Arcadian Valley, where they came from, there were three types of magic. Physical magic was the type that often allowed fire balls and even teleportation; mental magic allowed mind reading and manipulation; and nature magic, which allowed for healing and control over plants, animals, and weather. There was much more to it than that, he explained, but these were the basics.

"We had all assumed this was the case everywhere, until those of us from the temple began traveling," he went on, "and came across the folks such as Lady Estair here. To see that magic manifested itself differently in other parts of the world truly amazes me."

"Take, for example," Larick cut in, "the magic that we hear your paladins can perform. This, in many ways, makes no sense to us. They can cast force fields, but also heal, as the Lady has demonstrated. This means the magic must be some mixture of physical and nature magic, as if the colors were mixed in the way the body accepts the magic."

"Or, as I've theorized," Volney interrupted, "that there's no base colors to begin with, but one large pot from which all magic is drawn."

"Either way," Larick said, casting a glare at his fellow mystic, "does any of this make sense?"

"Not in the slightest," came another voice, and they turned to see Alastar. He stood before Rhona, hand on the hilt of his sword. "Since what we do is *not* magic."

"Ah, the unbeliever," Larick said, eyes lighting up with excitement. "It's truly a pleasure."

"Unbeliever?" Alastar scoffed. "My faith is solid, sir."

"A different sort of faith," Larick said. "Where we come from, there's talk of a matriarch and patriarch, of old gods from the days of before." He waved as if dismissing all that for another time. "We've seen Estair's demonstration of her skills and would love for you to share with us what you think separates you from her."

His brow furrowed, and he looked from Rhona to Estair. "I think we've stayed long enough. Come, sister, let's thank these fine people for their hospitality and be on our way."

He had reached the exit before turning to see that she wasn't following.

"I'm... curious," she admitted. "Whatever this is, it's a part of me now. If I don't learn to control it, who knows what will happen next time."

She knew he wouldn't understand, so simply turned back to the mystics and said, "Let's try this."

"Rhona, these people, they're..." Alastar was at her side in a flash, pulling her arm. "They're..."

"What? Magic users? Evil?" She pulled her arm free and went over to stand by them. "If that's what you think, then say it. But know that you're saying the same about me!"

He glanced around, unsure of his next move, and Rhona noticed his eyes lingering on Estair longer than the others. Interesting! When he folded his arm and raised an eyebrow, she knew he wasn't going anywhere.

Larick must have sensed it, too, for he turned to Rhona and said, "Well then, let's try and coax that magic out of you, shall we? It would be easier if we had a little of the brew left that our order makes, but my brother here drank it all on our journey west."

"If I had known we were going to walk so damn far," Volney argued, "I would have brought more."

The first few minutes was spent with her simply trying to recreate what happened in the castle when they had been attacked. Soon others had joined them, including Donnon, they had come to watch. But nothing was happening.

"She ain't no mage," an older woman called from the crowd.

Larick rubbed his temple and then perked up and turned to Rhona. "Perhaps you need to feel that you're in danger."

His eyes went white and instantly he was gone, a large bear in his place.

"What madness is this?" Alastar demanded, rushing to her side and drawing his sword. The two were no longer in the sinkhole, but atop a cliff with waves crashing far below.

She shrieked as the bear approached, but Alastar swung with his sword, shouting, "Back, stay back!"

"This... this can't be real," Rhona said. But the taste of the salty wind and the way it whipped her gown across her body certainly felt real. The cold chilled her bones, and when she tripped and her head was over the edge of the cliff, she had no doubt that if she fell, it would all be over.

"I told you they were evil!" he shouted.

The bear reared up on its hind legs and charged, roaring the whole way.

Alastar prayed and, as his eyes turned gold, a barrier of light formed between them and the bear.

But the bear charged right through it!

If that bear hit him, they'd both be going over the cliff. Rhona couldn't let that happen.

She stood, grabbed onto Alastar, and with a blink of her eyes, the two had formed into shadows that zipped out of the way of the bear and appeared on the other side of it.

They reformed back into themselves and were left gasping, sucking in great gasps of air. Rhona's lungs felt like they had been twisted up, completely emptied and just now refilling with air, and her muscles and entire body ached, but the move had been successful. The bear's momentum pushed it on and, even as it turned to process what had happened, it fell over the edge with a mighty roar.

Their surroundings vanished, replaced instead with the sinkhole they had been in moments before.

Larick stumbled as if punched, and then recovered to join the others in staring at Rhona in shock.

"By the light, what the hell just happened?" Alastar demanded. He spun, turning his sword on the mystics. "You tried to kill us!"

Volney held up his hands to show he meant no harm. "It was simply an illusion, meant to pull out the emotions that would cause your sister's magic to be demonstrated. Neither of you were in any danger, I assure you."

"The better question," Larick said, eyes fixed on Rhona, "was how did you do that? It wasn't a true teleportation. It was like…"

"She became one with the shadows," Estair finished the thought for him.

"I don't know," Rhona muttered, then stumbled and Alastar had to catch her. "It was like, my instincts took over. One minute I wanted nothing more than for the two of us to be out of that bear's path, the next, we were."

Alastar's eyes were still wide with the shock of it, but he nodded and added, "It was glorious."

That hadn't been the word she'd expected from him.

Horrible, maybe, or evil. Anything negative, really. He put his hand on her forehead and closed his eyes, and a moment later she felt the familiar warmth of a paladin's healing touch her.

"Come," Alastar said, leading his sister away. "I think that's enough demonstration for now."

The others made room, and Rhona was glad to see them gone. While her body was healed, and she could walk on her own, her mental energy had been quite drained by the whole ordeal. All she wanted to do was lie back down and sleep again.

Donnon couldn't sleep, so he found himself exploring the caverns, a small flame hovering over his outstretched hand. It wasn't the first time he'd been in a place like this, but he had never been in these exact ones. Everything in him said they needed to leave immediately, that each moment he sat here was time wasted.

But he knew they had to shake the sorcerers, and needed to be healed. If they weren't able to achieve those two goals, all of this would be for nothing.

While the others healed, he'd be tormented with his need to rush, to return home. And in the meantime, try to distract himself with the oddities he might find down here, such as the sign he found buried in the dirt that read, "ic school library." They were familiar with the concept of schools, but in his clan, it was all done via tutors, gathering children together in groups of three or four and working to learn. Those who knew farming would work to improve their farming knowledge, those who had an ability to do magic would focus on magic.

Why any school would need a library was beyond him. And an "ic" library seemed more confusing, though, he supposed that was either an acronym or the other letters had worn off.

He continued down a dark tunnel, the flame flickering brighter when he needed more light.

When he came to a dead end where the roof came steadily down, he crouched and looked to see if there were any hidden treasures, and sighed when he found none. Not that he had expected to find any.

Then he froze, at the reflection of the flame to his left. When he leaned in, he saw it was a piece of glass at an angle, an old window or something. He moved the flame aside and let it die down slightly, realizing he could see through the window… and then he saw her and couldn't help but stare.

Rhona.

She looked so beautiful in her sleep. During the day, she was exciting and not bad to look at, but he didn't realize until this moment that she was truly a sight for the eyes.

Of course, sometimes people become more beautiful as you get to know them. A completely plain woman might become stunning after a day spent laughing together. But he was mostly sure that wasn't the case here, or not entirely. Her red, almost strawberry hair spread out around her head in a way that made her look like she was floating, her soft, pale skin offset by the rosiness of her cheeks and lips that pouted slightly.

He stared, wondering what she was dreaming of, until a clearing of someone's throat came from behind him.

With a jump that caused him to hit his head on the dirt above, he spun and saw Larick, the mystic, standing there.

"This is part of your mating ritual in the Lost Isles?" Larick said with a chuckle.

"No, I wasn't—"

"Oh come now, young clansman." Larick smiled, and his eyes flashed white. "You're talking to a mystic, a reader of minds."

"Oh… shite."

Larick chuckled. "Though, I must admit, when I saw you there, I expected fairly dirty thoughts. What's wrong with you?"

Now, it was Donnon's turn to laugh, though, he caught himself and stepped away from the window, so as not to be too loud and wake Rhona below. "You mean, why am I not having more perverted thoughts when staring through a window at a sleeping woman?"

The man nodded.

"Let's just say I have the utmost respect for women. I've had too many great ones in my life to think otherwise."

Larick smiled and gave him a nod. "I respect that, clansman."

"You can call me Donnon."

"Of course, I can. I'd rather call you pervert-who-watches-sleeping-women, but you took the fun away from that one by being such a nice guy."

Donnon waved him off with a smile. "Aye, but you haven't explained what you're doing here, eh? For all I know, you already found this spot and were about to earn your nickname for yourself."

"I assure you, I wasn't. But, since you can't read minds…" Larick shrugged. "Perhaps we can walk back, and you can tell me a bit more of your ways in the clans? I know Volney would be pleased to take notes, for the records we hope to keep of our journeys."

"Spill my secrets to complete strangers?" Donnon pursed his lips, considering this. "Why the hell not?"

So, they started walking, and soon met Volney, and as they did, Donnon told them about the elemental spirits they see as kids. How, when a member of a clan first sees a spirit, they report in to the clan elders. They are then given a coming of age ceremony of sorts, no longer considered a child once they are able to wield magic, regardless of the age. But they wouldn't be given the title of water, fire, or wind mage, based on the respective clans, until they had moved beyond the stage where a spirit guided them in their use of magic.

For a moment, they looked at him like they knew something he didn't, but neither said a thing. When they reached the kitchen, he found a drink and a taste of apple tart, and went on to explain the differences between the clans, and how they had formed over the years, happy to have the distraction. His clan, for example, had gone to the mountains and found their affinity for fire magic early on. Some, such as the water clan his best childhood friend had belonged to, didn't even realize they knew magic for a few years after the end of the Age of Madness.

Then the paladins came, led by their High Paladin, Sir Gildon, preaching about magic being evil. But the clans all knew that what he did was no different than their magic. Sure, it performed differently, but his eyes changed color and miraculous events occurred. As far as they were concerned, there was no question about it being magic, and therefore none of the clans ever even considered that they might be evil.

"Rightly so," Larick said, and then continued with the questioning as the hours went on, while Volney scribbled away at his parchment.

CHAPTER EIGHT

After leaving Rhona to nap, Alastar went to grab a snack and inquire about bathing. The mystic, Volney, sat in a chair scribbling on parchment. The man gave Alastar a brief nod, then continued writing.

"This Arcadian Valley," Alastar started, "what makes it so special that you'd come here to *teach* us?"

Volney paused, wrote one last word, and then looked up at him. "Perhaps I've given the wrong idea. We're here to learn as much as to teach. Consider it a joint information exchange."

Alastar bit into an apple and considered that for a moment, then swallowed and said, "What do you hope to learn from us?"

"First, let me ask you about magic. Your Order of Rodrick believes it to be evil, aye?"

"Naturally."

"Yes, naturally… But have you ever studied it? Bothered to ask where it came from?"

Alastar shook his head.

"What if I were to tell you that magic is really only fifty to a hundred years old?" Volney adjusted in his seat so that he could better face Alastar. "Give or take."

"We all know that it evolved at the end of the Age of Madness," Alastar said, annoyed. "This is nothing new. It only makes sense that it would be evil. First, dark forces turned much of the world into creatures no better than animals. Vile beasts. We defeated many of them, then fled, to the hills for the clans, the fortresses for my people. And then that madness transformed into magic."

"And how do you suppose that came into being?"

"Our beliefs tell us there must have been some form of intelligence behind it. Strike men mad, and when that doesn't work, give the evil among us great powers so that good might be defeated once and for all."

"Except, you no longer fully believe that, do you?" Volney leaned forward, eyes moving across Alastar's face, and then he smiled. "No, you do not."

Alastar frowned, wondering if the man was reading his mind. But no, that wasn't possible.

"Where I come from, we have a different tale of the coming of magic," Volney explained. "The simple, not entirely accurate version is that the Founder used magic to bring the Age of Madness to an end. Do some people use magic now for evil? I can attest to the fact that they do, most certainly. But only because magic has come to this world indiscriminately. It is not for the evil, not for the good. In fact, my understanding of it is that magic came about because of something called *the Etheric*, and *nanocytes* in our blood that affect us and our connection to the Etheric in odd ways."

"It sounds like you're speaking gibberish."

Volney chuckled. "Indeed, I would think the same if I were you."

"How does this help me? How does knowing this help me heal my sister, or put it right in my mind that I've been fighting magic users for so long now?"

"None of it does. What you can do with this information is up to you. But… I hope you will consider what it means for you going forward, not looking back at your past."

Alastar took a seat next to the man, then tore off a chunk of bread from the loaf between them. "Your kind has kept records of our world and its goings-on?"

"Yes, though, it's not complete. Hence me being here."

"Before the Age of Madness, these buildings and ruins we see remnants of. What do your records recall of that?"

Volney sighed and shook his head. "Little and less. The old ones who survived pass on stories they heard, of a time of regrowth after some catastrophic event that tore our world apart. Others speak of powerful beings from other worlds and great wars." He waved at the sky. "Perhaps it's all going on right now? But who can you believe? In times like this, when anything seems possible, it almost makes you believe every single story you hear."

"But not every story can be true." Alastar bit into the bread and chewed, then chased it with a gulp of apple cider. "Some talk of dragons, even of men and women who walked in the night and fed on blood. You have to draw the line somewhere."

"Indeed," Volney said, with a glint of humor in his eyes.

"You're not telling me something," Alastar said, eyes narrowed.

"Perhaps. But perhaps whatever I might tell you would only serve to throw more doubt into your mind."

Alastar shook his head and stood. "You're an odd one, there's no denying that fact, at least. Instead of sitting here and listening to your gibberish, I think I'll find myself a bath."

"A well needed one at that," Volney said with a wink and a hand wave in front of his nose.

"Yes, well, shall I apologize for being a man?"

"If all men here stink as you do, I'd think Roneland will face a population problem at some point."

"A true comedian." Alastar turned to the various passages. "One who knows where the baths would be, I hope?"

Volney pointed him in the right direction, and Alastar was glad to be done with him. Still, what he said certainly warranted consideration. If magic had truly been the cure to the Age of Madness, everything he had been raised to believe would be thrown into the gutters with the rest of the sewage.

He wondered what the High Paladin would have to say about all of this—if he was still alive.

He soon found the room where they had brought in hot water, anticipating his desire. Once alone, he stripped and lowered himself into the tub with a long sigh of relief. The last time it had felt this good to take a bath had been after a raid, his first, when he had nearly been killed. His brother in arms, Sir Taland, had stepped in to defend him then, blocking a burst of flame with his shield of light, taking down the fire mage with his sword.

Ever since that moment, Alastar had been intent on spiritual study, so that he would never again have to rely on a fellow paladin's defense to save his life.

Now, he had much bigger worries than himself—there was no denying that his sister was a witch, or some form of magic user.

If there was one fact he was certain of, it was that his sister was in no way evil. Unfortunately, there was no way the other paladins would ever see it that way.

So, the question was what to do next.

He leaned back so that his head rested on the edge of the tub, and closed his eyes. As it seemed to him, they could disappear and never be seen again. That seemed the easiest option, but also the cowardly one. The oath he had sworn in the castle could not be ignored—he was duty bound to serve the Order of Rodrick and bring peace to this land.

But maybe there was some room for maneuvering within that vow. Would going after the Sword of Light in any way violate it? He didn't think so. What mattered now was retrieving the sword so that he could unite the paladins and bring this land to peace.

He wasn't sure how long he had been lying there, when he sensed a presence. A warmth came over him, and he felt hands running across his body, but when he came spluttering up, he saw no hands—only a warm glow of light moving across his body.

Estair stood in the entryway, biting her lower lip to keep from laughing. "I'd come closer, but wouldn't want to spoil your innocence," she said and then pretended to crane her neck for a peek.

"What… was that?" he asked, and then ran his hand through the golden light that hadn't left him.

"Once you embrace that this isn't some blessing from a saint, but actual magic, you'll find it much more malleable."

"Is that so?" He sat straight, only then realizing he hadn't thought about ensuring he had a towel, or even clean clothes, for that matter.

"Don't worry." Estair motioned behind her, and a young woman entered carrying both. "You'd be surprised how well prepared we clansfolk can be."

The young woman set the clothes down beside the tub and then held out the towel for Alastar. He expected them both to leave, but neither did. With a frown, he accepted the towel and stood with his rear to them as he dried.

"She has a gift, your sister," Estair said, ignoring the nudity. "You realize that now, correct?"

"I do." He glanced over his shoulder as he wrapped the towel around his waist and stepped from the tub. "But I'm still trying to figure out how to process it."

She nodded, and he noticed her eyes move across his abs. The other woman was looking at him, too, and he frowned.

"Is this how all of you always are?" he asked. "A man bathes, and you come for the show?"

"You can leave," Estair said to the other woman, then laughed. "Just my idea of teasing a paladin. You're the first we've had, honestly. It's quite fun."

"And if I were to simply drop my towel here and take you up on your offer?"

She blushed, but shrugged.

He saw it as the bluff it was, but had his dignity and respect for a woman, so instead kept the towel on and bent down to pick up the clothes he'd been brought.

"These… are the clothes of a clansman," he said, standing and holding up the black pants and tunic.

"At least it's not a kilt," she said, and then turned her back to him.

"Leaving so soon?"

"Simply giving you privacy while you change."

"Wow, so you are capable of decency." He said as he slipped into the pants. "I wouldn't have believed it."

"It's all relative," she said, turning back as he finished pulling the shirt down. "Compared to the ladies of the court, or even the paladin castles, I imagine I'm downright scandalous. But compared to some of the women you'll meet in the highlands… I'm a kitten."

"A kitten?"

"I'll purr and play with a ball, but I'm hardly in heat."

He just shook his head at that and said, "Wow, okay. Wow."

She laughed and said, "Come, let's get you supplied and get on our way."

"You really mean to come with us then?"

She nodded, but they were just out the door when she froze at the sound of a low whistle. He turned to ask what that was, but her expression told enough. Her eyes were wild, her lips pulled back into a snarl as if she were about to attack.

"We're under attack," she said.

"Who?"

"The mystics will know," she said and nodded for him to follow. They ran through the tunnels until they were back in the dining area, where Rhona, Donnon, and the two mystics waited.

A second later, Lokane entered. He had a broadsword strapped to his back and held a second sword that he tossed to Estair.

It was only then that Alastar noticed Larick's white eyes.

"What's he doing?" Rhona asked, only giving Alastar's odd clothing a sideways glance.

"Scouting," Lokane said, pointing above.

A moment later the mystic's eyes returned to normal, only they were wide with fear. "It's them, the sorcerers. I don't know how, but your base has been discovered and is under siege.

CHAPTER NINE

Rhona stumbled back, a piercing pain shooting through her head as the trees surrounding her vanished and were replaced with images of their attackers.

Arms wrapped around her. A voice asked if she was feeling ill, but then the pain came again, flashes of red and black with their faces—snarling, evil faces. One stood out from the others—a man with long, blond hair, his eyes white.

When the images stopped, she realized it had all been a vision.

It was Donnon who held her, Estair nearby now with her eyes glowing gold. A flash of light crossed between Rhona and the ceiling like a shimmer across a pond, and then Estair's eyes returned to normal.

"That should hold them from doing more of… whatever that was," Estair said, then turned and shouted. "All hands, into the tunnels!"

"What's the plan?" Alastar asked, being sure to first cast

a glance in Donnon's direction that made it clear he was to get his hands off of Rhona.

"Can we fight them?" Donnon asked, glancing at the torches nearby.

"And send this whole place up in flames?" Estair shook her head. "Can you imagine a tunnel full of fire? Anyone without your powers would be burnt to a crisp."

"What do you propose then?"

Estair licked her lip as she eyed them all. "As much as I hate to say it, we retreat. Move to a fighting position in the hills and then, if they're still on our tails, we stand our ground."

"The fortress of Stirling ought to hold," Lokane said. "Make it so."

With a wave of her hand, Estair led the way through one of the tunnels.

"Fortress of Stirling?" Volney asked.

"An old castle on a cliff," Alastar answered. "One from the old days, even before the Age of Madness, if you can believe it. Partially destroyed, but rebuilt stronger than ever by the clans. It's one of the only locations this far south they've been able to hold, well, or so we thought." He gestured at their surroundings. "It seems there was a lot we were unaware of."

"If we go there and they find out my brother's a paladin," Rhona said to Estair, "they'll see him burned alive. Can you guarantee his safety there?"

"As a paladin?" She shook her head. "It's as you say, with some of the clans. Others, such as ours, less so. Which is why, Alastar, you must do your best to say nothing remotely paladin-like while we're there."

Rhona could tell by the flash of anger in his eyes that the request wasn't well received, and she knew why. This was tantamount to blasphemy as far as the Order of Rodrick was concerned. But didn't he understand that such a way of thinking was quickly being disproven? He had to see it this way because otherwise, it meant he still saw her in a way she could never accept.

"If we even make it to the fortress," Lokane said as they turned down a dark tunnel they were only able to see by the glow of Estair's spell. She held her hand out in front like a torch, light emanating from it softly.

"I'm glad for your eternal optimism," Estair said with a glare.

Lokane nodded, glancing around at the men and women who were piling in from various tunnels and joining them as they made the retreat.

"Don't do what I think you're considering," Estair said. "It's best to stick together."

"It'd be best to see that as many of us make it to the Fortress of Stirling as possible."

"Not at the risk of their leader's life," she argued.

He seemed to consider for a moment, then said, "And yet, a leader must be willing to make these decisions." With that, he broke off from the main group and whistled. Men and women from the group wearing a darker green than the rest broke off to join him.

"His personal guard and our most elite fighting force," Estair explained as they continued to hurry along, noticing Rhona's glance back. "They'll move to another location to distract and hold off the attack."

"He'd sacrifice himself for our safety?" Rhona asked.

"Let's hope it doesn't come to that. These sorcerers, they're not ours, and they'd see us burn as fast as they'd kill your brother and take you for your magic."

"And the other paladins?" Rhona asked as they ran.

"They will be dealt with in their own time."

Each turn sent Rhona's heart into a new flutter until she was sure it was going to explode if this didn't end soon. If it weren't for the fact that she was surrounded by mages, two mystics, and her brother, she would have likely curled up into a ball right there. Except, then there was the fact that she was now somehow performing incredibly powerful magic, too. She wasn't sure how it happened exactly, but she knew that, so far, when she was backed into a corner it had come to her aid.

In fact, she realized, those bastards had better stay the hell out of her way.

When they turned into a wider passage that led out into daylight, she was smiling, almost hoping they would run into trouble, so that she could see the sorcerers get their butts kicked.

That didn't help her nerves, though, when they crested the incline and found a small army of crazed looking men standing before them. Their eyes were wide and wild, their arms muscular, and they held crude weapons that included everything from metal spikes, crude swords that were chipped and worn, to hatchets, and even pitchforks.

"Remnant!" Volney cried, pulling to a halt.

"Rem-what?" Rhona hissed as the army of so-called remnant began to process these new arrivals. Then she recalled that name, described by stories in the castle of a people far to the west, on the island of Sair Talem.

"They're nearly mindless, focused on violence and not much else. If the sorcerers are somehow controlling them, we're in for more of a challenge than I anticipated."

"We?" Rhona asked. "You're officially taking our side on this?"

"Against the likes of them? Most certainly."

"We'll need all the help we can get," Alastar said, and then bowed his head in prayer.

"Are you seriously still doing it that way?" Estair said, lifting her glowing hand up and doubling her spell so that the light flowed out from her and over the others. Rhona felt her muscles become more alert, ready for a fight.

"It's the only way I know how," Alastar said, finishing his prayer. When he looked up again, his eyes glowed gold along with his sword, and he smiled. "Let's move them out of our way."

He led the charge, while behind him others drew swords and bows and arrows. Three fire mages drew flint and lit the torches they had brought with them, then took up defensive positions.

Already, the remnant army was charging, letting out a great roar. Alastar's sword gleamed as he cut through one after another, and the clansmen and women were doing their part. The remnant numbers were large, though, and a group broke through on the left.

That's when the fire mages came into play, casting a wall of fire that rose up between themselves and their attackers. Half the remnant buckled and ran back toward Alastar while the others were cut down in the process.

The rest ran right through the flames! Many of those

fell in balls of fire, but others were coming right for the mages.

"Watch this," Volney said at Rhona's shoulder, pointing at them. "Once the fire takes hold, the mages have full control."

The woman mage stepped forward, twisting her hands before her, and then lifted them into the air as if heaving a massive weight. Instantly, the flaming remnant were lifted into the air and thrown back into the rear ranks, spreading the fire farther.

What resulted was a panic in the back ranks of the remnant, a crazed rage at the front. They were throwing themselves at Alastar and the others now, while the rest of them were running around in chaos.

One broke through, a flaming wild-man with a hatchet coming straight for Rhona. One of the mages turned and lifted his hand to send the remnant slamming into the wall so that its head exploded on impact.

Damn, Rhona thought as she watched. Once those flames hit you, the fire mages had a huge advantage.

The pain in her head returned along with the flash of that man's face—white eyed and all, and then a new figure appeared at the rear of the remnant. A bald head like the mystics, but she recognized him from the paladin castle before it had fallen—one of the strange sorcerers

He waved his hands and pushed forward, sending a cascade of water across the burning remnant and over the torches even, so that the fire mages were rendered powerless.

As everyone recovered, some slipping on the now damp

ground, he stepped forward and began to move his arms again. The other two sorcerers appeared behind him, and then the figure with the blond hair and white eyes, leering at Rhona.

"You!" Alastar said as he regained his footing and held his sword at the ready.

"Address me as High Master Irdin, young lady," he said, clearly addressing Rhona and ignoring the rest. "Consider this your initiation to the most powerful army this world has ever seen. All you need do is bow."

"Bow?" She shook her head. "Not going to happen."

"I'm giving you the chance to become one of us. To let your friends here walk away unharmed… for now."

She looked at Estair and the others, and lastly, her brother. Every single one of them had fight in their eyes. They wouldn't allow it any more than she would be willing to go along with this sorcerer's demands.

The audacity of this man, to threaten every one of them. These people who had taken her in and treated her like one of their own, without any expectation of anything in return.

Many of these clansmen and women lay injured from the short battle, all because of her coming here. That got to her most of all.

"Go to hell," she said, and was pleased to see the sorcerer's eyes go wide at the sight of her stepping forward and the shadows around her dancing across the walls as they converged on her hands, twisting like a dark whirlpool in the air.

"Last chance," he said. "You continue down this path,

you'll find only death and destruction. With us, you can have everything you've ever wanted!"

Her voice came out harsh, echoing as she said, "You honestly think I couldn't just take it?"

"Rhona, don't!" Alastar shouted, but it was too late.

With a laughter that sounded like it came from ten of her, echoing from some place she didn't recognize, she spread her arms wide, and the shadows spread out from her. Shadows took her, and she was darting among the remnant and sucking any sign of life from them. The only reason they didn't get to the sorcerers, too, was that one of them had waved his hands as the others converged on him, and then all were gone, teleported elsewhere.

As the last of the remnant fell, lifeless, Rhona, too, collapsed. She had known it was coming, but didn't expect the pain that came this time. In an instant, Alastar and Estair were on her, casting healing light and protective charms, but the pain was internal, pushing its way out.

She clenched her fists and heard someone screaming, then registered her nails digging into someone's hand. Her teeth burned, she was clenching them so hard, and then, with a final prayer from her brother, the feeling was gone.

Only, this time he fell at her side, barely able to hold himself up. Estair looked weak, too, but other warriors quickly came to their aid and helped them to stand.

"Quick," Estair said, "get us out of here."

The warriors obeyed, grabbing them under the arms and helping them to run and continue their retreat. They emerged into a field with a large cliff in the distance, a castle at its top, tall hills around to the other side.

But more remnant were on the field, running all out to converge on their position.

"Get us to the castle," Estair said.

They ran, but it looked hopeless. Using magic, it seemed, took its toll. She wondered if this was it, and her steps began to slow. That is, until a small group of warriors in dark green burst forth from a passage hidden by rocks, and tore through the nearest wave of remnant.

"Go!" Lokane commanded, and turned with his cadre of defenders to take on the next wave.

"You heard him!" Estair shouted, and they ran.

A warrior moved to his side to help them, while a vanguard led the charge, slicing and kicking until their path was clear. They soon reached a rocky ledge, which they climbed onto with ease. They were running along a worn-down street with ruins of buildings that looked to hold some remains of the days before madness, though the fortress was at the end of the path.

New clansmen, dressed in an odd assortment of blues and white, in what looked more like dress uniforms, ran out to greet the new arrivals. Their eyes went black as they formed a line and, as one, pushed out with their hands. It was as if an invisible wall appeared, with many remnant slamming into it and falling back upon themselves.

Rhona and the others passed the blue-clad clansmen, and then the invisible wall blew out, and she realized it had been a strong wind, not a wall at all.

"Stay with me," Alastar said as he ran alongside Rhona, barely able to keep going, but for their strength, pushed on by the adrenaline pumping through their veins. Donnon had his strength, too, as he rushed to join the two of them with a simple nod.

One last sprint to the gates, and they were almost there before a blast of ice spears rained down on them. A clansman was able to push against the wind, so that the spears missed their mark, but one still pierced Estair in the thigh. She fell with a cry, and Alastar went back for her.

Rhona tried to go back for him, but Donnon grabbed her arm.

"He can fend for himself," Donnon shouted as he pulled her onward and through the gates.

The rest of the clansmen were joining them behind the gates, while two of them focused on keeping the ice off because, although they were inside the fortress gates, they still weren't under cover.

"Where's my brother?" Rhona shouted, spinning around, looking for him. She was about to run back out through the closing gates, when she heard him calling her name. She turned to see him and Estair making their way for the interior keep, and rushed over to join them.

Others joined them as well, and soon, they had the doors shut and secured. The sounds of winds and ice, plus the occasional shout of a remnant or fighter falling could be heard.

Rhona found a seat at the table in the center of the room, and sat, her legs shaking.

"What the hell was that?" a broad-shouldered clansman clad in blue and white demanded as he strode into the room. He looked to Estair first, who was sitting, looking intently at Alastar with wide eyes that seemed to be trying to communicate something that Rhona didn't understand at first, but as Alastar wasn't making any attempt to heal the woman, she got the gist. *Don't use any paladin powers here, or it could mean his life.*

But the woman was bleeding, so Rhona figured she only had one thing she could do. She stepped forward, mouth open as if to answer, and promptly fainted.

CHAPTER TEN

The room's attention had suddenly moved to Rhona, so Alastar quickly bowed his head and ran his hand over Estair's thigh, just briefly, enough to make sure it wasn't too badly wounded without raising suspicion.

As far as he could tell when he looked up, no one had noticed.

He was ninety percent sure his sister had caused the diversion on purpose, but since he wasn't completely certain, he now ran to her side to check on her, maneuvering his way through the others.

She opened her eyes with a groan, and Alastar recognized that look in her eyes. Definitely a charade for his benefit. He helped her to stand, but when he turned, the large man in blue and white stood before them.

"And who might these two be?" the man asked.

"They're with us," Lokane said. A path cleared to show him standing there, covered in blood, his team behind him. "A special type of guest."

"Indeed, they would have to be to bring this sort of power against us."

"Master Garrett," Estair said, standing feebly. "We apologize, but knew our only chance for survival was to come here. She… has something they want."

"They?" His eyes narrowed. "The sorcerers of Gallant?"

Estair nodded. "We suspect so. But, they seem to have a teleporter. Why aren't they in here with us now?"

"That would be us," Volney said with a wave. "Hello. Larick and Volney, mystics of the Arcadian Valley, at your service."

Larick had his eyes whited out, but he waved.

"Forgive my colleague," Volney said. "He's engaged in blocking the teleporter's mind from being able to target this fortress with his magic."

"Does that mean Larick's power's stronger?"

"No, which is why we must hurry with the next phase of this plan." Volney joined the rest to look at Master Garrett, then Lokane, and back again. Nobody seemed certain who would make the call here.

Rhona stepped forward. "I saw one…"

"We all did," Estair said, looking at her confused.

"No, I mean, the one with the white in his eyes. I had a vision of him."

"Ah," Volney stood and approached her, then paused, looking around the room. "Some of you might not yet be aware of the power of mystics, or magic that controls the mind. It can be used in many ways, including, it would seem, tracking down Rhona."

Rhona gave a half-wave. "That's me."

"You're sure of this?" Estair asked.

Rhona nodded. "I'm definitely Rhona. Oh, and that I saw him? Aye."

Alastar chuckled. "You always were the type to make dumb jokes when it's time to be serious."

She couldn't deny that, and didn't want to voice her next concern, but had to know. "It's when I use magic, isn't it?"

"What?" the master of the fortress demanded. "What're you talking about?"

But Volney had a cryptic look on his face, one of confusion mixed with determination. "The only way to get them away from here is if you use magic somewhere else."

"And since they have a teleporter," Larick added, "they'd be there in an instant."

"We could lure them away, in theory. But if they didn't find her, they'd likely assume it was some sort of a trick and return to attack here."

"They might do that anyway, simply for harboring her."

This got the attention of Master Garrett, but after a moment of shock and clenched fists, he noticed everyone looking at him and bellowed out, "*What?* You think this is the first time the Fortress of Stirling has been under attack? I'd turn over a girl rather than fight?" He laughed a hearty laugh. "Any of you think that, you clearly don't know Master Garrett or the Stirling Guard."

A sound that seemed to be half war-cry, half grunt went up from the clansfolk in the room.

"You plan your escape, or whatever the hell you want to do, while me and mine will stage the defense." He turned to Lokane and waited, one eyebrow raised.

"Deal," Lokane agreed. "If we can make it to the tunnels and head north, we just might have a shot at—"

"No," Rhona said, catching even Alastar off-guard.

"Excuse me, no?" Lokane frowned. "What do you mean, no?"

"I mean, my brother has his mission, and I mean to see he achieves it."

"Whatever mission you think you had no longer seems like the priority here, at least not at the moment." Lokane gestured to the room. "These people's lives are at stake as well as your own."

Alastar stepped up next to his sister. "She's right. And what we must do now is for the good of all here. We will retrieve the Sword of Light, and be unstoppable."

"If you use magic, they find you," Estair said. "So, we must be on the move. We cannot risk them finding us here."

Alastar assessed the room. These people were fighters, that much was plain. But they were also scared. Whatever forces the sorcerers were playing with, it wasn't normal. He couldn't let them fall into harm's way.

"We'll be going on our own," the paladin said.

"Like hell you are!" Estair said. "They want your sister for her magic, and you'd walk out there and give it to them?"

"No, we'd walk out and distract them from this place, and then be on the move. We get the sword, then go after them. Ensure they never hurt anyone ever again."

"I don't suppose anyone here knows how to teleport?" Rhona asked.

The rest shook their heads.

Volney looked at his companion, then shook his head. "I'm not surprised. We haven't heard of anyone being able to do it outside of the Arcadian Valley until now."

"Here's a crazy idea," Rhona said. "Can you project something into another's mind?"

Volney hesitated, but nodded. "Depending on the power of the other mind."

"This other mystic, or whatever he is that they have… Could you trick him into believing I was elsewhere using my magic?"

"With the power he seems to have, it's doubtful," Volney offered.

"But not impossible," Larick argued.

"At best, we'd be able to put the image in his mind for a matter of minutes, maybe only seconds."

"That might be all we'd need," Alastar said. "If we can divert their attention long enough for the two of us to make a run for it, we can break through their ranks and, by the time they figure it out, be long gone."

"That's too great a risk," Lokane said.

"It might not be." Rhona held up a hand, focusing, and all light disappeared from it for a moment. "Since the last time I used magic, I've felt a change in my body, like I've only just learned to breathe. When my magic was put against theirs the last couple of times, mine was superior."

"It also drained you, and fast," Alastar pointed out. "If you rely too much on this… power, or whatever you want to call it, how do you know it won't kill you?"

She shook her head. "It's part of me, I know that now."

He knew that look in his sister's eyes, when she became determined. When she set her mind to something, the only person who had ever been able to talk her out of it had been their mother. Now, he knew there was only one option.

"It's as my sister says." Alastar's face held steady, and the company knew he meant it.

"Then my team and I will lead the charge," Lokane said. "We'll have the wind mages give us a head start, and then we'll get you as far as we can before turning back."

"Thank you," Rhona said, nodding.

"You'd let this happen?" Estair demanded of Garrett. "You'd let this poor girl run out into those dangers, when you could protect her in this fortress?"

He frowned at the idea, his eyes roaming over Alastar and Rhona. "First of all, I have families here. We must stop the attack, before they are hurt. I believe this young lady might just be capable of what she says. The power within… I sense it unlike anything I've ever felt before. Second, I won't harbor his kind." His eyes rested on Alastar. "No fighters of mine will die in defense of a paladin."

Alastar reached for his sword, but Estair darted over to stand between the two, limping on her injured leg. "What gave him away?"

Garrett laughed. "We've been fighting paladins as long as I can remember. You think I don't recognize that look of contempt in his eyes?"

"I assure you, sir," Alastar said, "whatever misgivings I may have once held toward your kind are rapidly being replaced by respect and admiration."

"Unfortunately, I can't say the same for you." Garrett dismissed him with a wave of his hand. "If the paladin wants to throw himself to the wolves, so be it. And dammit, Estair, heal your leg already, or let him do it. I'll not raise arms against him, not under these conditions, so you can all stop pretending."

"We were all drained after the fight to get here," she said, but nodded to Alastar. "If you're feeling up to it."

He glared at Garrett as he approached her and knelt. Head bowed, he said a quick prayer. When he looked up, the leg was healing and a room full of hate-filled eyes focused on him. They had lost too many of their brothers and sisters over the years to the magic wars to be okay with him being there, performing blessings such as this.

"We go as soon as we can," he said.

"Let it be so." Garrett turned to one of his lieutenants and said, "I want them equipped, fully prepared for the journey ahead. Let it not be said that we sent these two to their deaths without preparing them first."

"Three," Donnon said.

"Excuse me?"

"I need to return to my clan. I came for a healer, and, it would seem, I have one, if Alastar will come with me."

"And lead the sorcerers right to your doorstep?" Garrett shook his head. "That's your funeral you're asking for."

"Not if we make it undiscovered. It's well worth the risk."

"What could be worth bringing the wrath of these sorcerers down upon your people?"

Donnon gulped, his eyes revealing the fact that he had a

difficult time answering that, but with a sideways glance toward Rhona finally said, "It's my daughter."

Alastar noted the frown that crossed Rhona's face, but there was something not adding up that pulled at his attention. "A man's love for his daughter is strong, I can only imagine. But worth risking the entire clan over?"

"If there was a clan left, that might be a question worth considering," Donnon replied. "But it's worse than you think. My little Kia, she… has the black marks."

"The plague…" Estair took a deep breath. "The clan has abandoned you two?"

"All but two of them, who I fear will have contracted the plague by the time I return. If I don't have a healer with me, all three will likely die."

"Then it's settled," Rhona said, answering for all of them.

Alastar nodded. "It's settled."

He had heard of this plague spreading throughout the highlands. There was even talk among the Order of Rodrick that it was the Saint sending down punishment on the magic users.

How could he accept that now, though? Now that his sister was one of them, and these people who had risked their lives for theirs were, too?

One thing was clear now—these men and women were no longer his enemy, and if he could repay them for the assistance they had provided, he certainly would.

Garrett nodded to his lieutenant, who had not yet moved, but now scampered off to carry out the order. Next, the large man turned to Alastar and Rhona and said,

"If you pull this off, the next time we meet will be as friends."

Alastar gave him a curt nod. "Let's hope we pull it off then."

In the silence that followed, the howling winds mixed with pounding and shrieks from the remnant, and Alastar felt his hand clenching and unclenching as he wished to run out and take his sword to as many of those beasts as he could.

The sooner the better, in his opinion. When the lieutenant returned and said they were ready for him, he nodded to the room and was glad to put it behind him.

He, Rhona, and Donnon followed the man through passages that smelled of old wood, rattled with icy bursts that made their way in past the wind spells. They stopped when they reached the armory, where the lieutenant fitted Alastar with leather plates complete with pauldrons for the shoulders and arms, and a tasset belt with a hanging plate to protect the groin.

"Nothing... stronger?" Alastar asked.

The lieutenant shook his head. "Not that you'd be able to run in."

"Good point."

They fitted Rhona in similar attire, though, better made for a woman. She looked the highlander warrior part, with her leather armor over the green dress, now taken in to allow for better running. The lieutenant fitted them each with plaid cloaks that hung over their shoulders to protect them from the cold during the day, and to be used as blankets at night. Alastar cringed at the idea of wearing plaid, but was glad to see it was at least a neutral brown and green, not likely to associate him with any of the major clans who were in ongoing wars with the Order of Rodrick, should any of them have survived.

Donnon had already been equipped, but found himself two flame swords, as he called them, looking over them with awe. Each had a handle that shone with gold and a blade that curved up to the end, so that it resembled an arc of flame. He said the swords must've been recovered from one of his kin.

"Aye, they were," the lieutenant said. "We've had a few members of Clan Buchan join us in raids over the years. More than one fell along the way."

Donnon swung one of the blades and then strapped on the sheaths so that he could take both with him. "I won't be falling anytime soon, you can count on that. Not with these two companions at my back."

"At your side," Rhona corrected him.

The lieutenant grunted.

"Do you have a problem with this situation?" Alastar asked.

Ignoring him, the lieutenant kept his eyes on Donnon as he said, "You'd never see me putting my life in the hands of a paladin. Especially not the life of my daughter, if I had one."

"If you had one," Donnon said, "you would soon realize that you would do *anything* to protect her. Anything. Add to that the fact that these two have proven themselves more than once, and I would have to question anyone's intelligence to not trust them."

The lieutenant huffed and walked from the room,

pausing in the doorway to say, "For your sake, I hope you're right."

After he had left, Donnon smiled at the two, hands on his two sword hilts, and said, "I know I am."

"We'll get to your daughter and do what we can," Rhona said, and Alastar nodded in agreement.

"Then let's get out there and kick some remnant butt."

CHAPTER ELEVEN

It was weird, smelling the scent of death and hearing the sounds of warfare before the real fighting had even begun. Rhona stood at the top of the castle walls. Spells of fire and wind that the mages created flew out to attack the remnant, laying siege to the walls below. Whenever one fell, two more seemed to rise up in their place.

"Where are they all coming from?" Donnon asked in amazement.

"My best bet?" Alastar shouted over the winds. "They've come across from Sair Talem."

Rhona's heart clenched at the thought. She had heard stories about the people who still remained on the large island to the west, men and women whose recovery after the Age of Madness had left them in a state of constant ferocity, and a lust for death and destruction.

"What matters now isn't how they got here," Garrett said, standing behind them with an army of his wind mages in their blue and white colors, standing at the ready, "it's that you kill as many of the damned beasts as you can."

"We'll make them reconsider ever setting foot here again," Alastar said.

"If only they were capable of rational thought," Donnon said. "I fear we'll have to kill every last one of them if we ever hope to have a land free of remnant."

"Let's get started then," Alastar said, drawing his sword.

"You asked for it," Garrett said, and he raised a fist.

"Wait," Estair said, climbing the stairs to reach them. She came to Alastar and looked between him and Rhona. "If you ever need shelter or help, do not hesitate to come to me."

"Thank you," Alastar said, and to Rhona's surprise the woman gave him a hug and a kiss on the cheek.

Alastar blushed and kissed her hand.

"No kisses necessary," Rhona said when Estair looked her way, earning her a laugh from the woman. She shared a look of excitement with her brother.

Volney and Larick's eyes both went white and Volney said, "Now!"

The army of remnant below turned as one, like a swarm of bees homing in for their new target.

Garrett's fist pushed forward.

As one, his soldiers moved their hands in a circle and then motioned up and forward, as if lifting something into the air. Sure enough, the wind grabbed ahold of Alastar, Rhona, and Donnon, and carried them into the sky.

It was like they were flying, the wind soaring past, throwing them forward. Blasts of ice were pushed aside as an invisible fist broke through the sky and created a path for them, and then they were landing, the ground and the remnant coming up fast beneath.

"Swords at the ready!" Alastar shouted, and even Rhona had a dirk in one hand, a small shield in the other. It wasn't much, but she had figured it could be useful and was fairly lightweight.

Faces turned, teeth bared in snarls. She could see the red in their eyes, the glints of sunlight on their dull weapons, and then they hit the ground and the insanity began.

Lokane's squad of fighters landed off to the right, so that the remnant were thrown into a confused state. Alastar hacked through one after another of the marauding hoard, clearing a circle while Donnon clicked his flint rock, creating a wall of flame from just a spark that spread out before them, creating an opening in the ranks.

"GO!" he shouted, keeping the walls of fire on each side, but leaving a path clear through the middle for them to run through.

The stench of scorched remnant filled the air, the smoke choking Rhona as she ran. One of them pushed in through the flames, burning as it lifted its hatchet. It nearly had Rhona, but she hefted up the shield at her side and charged. She slammed it back into the flames, where it collapsed on its back, twitching once before she was past it, her chest thumping with the adrenaline and terror.

No, not terror, she realized. She was excited! Not only had she just survived the attack, she had kicked its butt!

While she was partly scared for her life, she almost wanted another one of them to attack her. She ran along behind Alastar, and then smiled at the sight of three remnant leaping over the backs of the others to reach them.

Donnon was stumbling in exhaustion from keeping the flames up, and Alastar had turned to fight another group of remnant that had fought their way through. This was up to Rhona.

With a smile, she let instinct take over and, as before, the shadows carried her. It was like one moment she was herself, the next she was a shadow darting through the air.

It was like she was barely there as she materialized long enough to tear out the throat of one of them, then was gone again before slamming into another. She was flying forward, her dirk cutting into the base of one's skull, blood splattering as she pulled the blade free.

And then she was back, wavering, and the knife flew out of her hands as the shadow took it, plunging the blade into the creature's chest. When the knife flew back to her, the shadow entered her and was gone.

The last of these three remnant fell to its knees, gone.

"The hell was that?" Donnon asked, having turned to see the tail end of the attack.

Problem was, he wasn't the only one to have noticed.

Using her magic had put the target back on her, and now all of the remnant were converging on her with fervor.

Not that she cared, as she watched the world take on a purple hue. She wavered, head spinning, but there were more of them. She let the shadow take her blade to the nearest attackers, and even before it had zipped through the necks of a dozen of them, she had burst into her shadow form and reappeared beside her brother.

He took her in with wide eyes, and said, "By all that is holy..."

She tried to say something, but zipped off again before he could answer, forming shadows at the feet of a group of remnant that absorbed them so that they sunk right through the ground and were gone. At the edge of the flames, she reappeared and grabbed the dirk from the air as it flew past, then spun and saw both Donnon and Alastar nearby.

The wind flew past her as she drifted into a shadow form that grabbed ahold of the two men, and then suddenly they were all three pulled free of the chaos that was the midst of the remnant.

She set them down at the outskirts of the rampaging horde, then lifted her hand to see what else this new magic could do. Her dress was torn, hanging in tatters, and her whole body was shaking uncontrollably. Blood dripped down her face, from her nose.

An army of remnant tilted before her, and a moment later the stony earth beneath her feet rose up to slam into her face.

With a moan, everything started to go black.

"Not so fast," Alastar said, hefting her up as a golden glow emanated from his hands and shone in his eyes.

"Get her out of here," Donnon said. "I'll hold them off!"

"You're coming with us," Alastar said, and sheathed his sword as he and Rhona helped each other to stand. "Otherwise, we'll never make it."

Donnon turned with a raised eyebrow, doubtful, but nodded. He released the flames, eyes turning back to normal, and ran as best he could to catch up with them.

"We're all weak," Alastar said. "We'll never make it!"

"I wouldn't be so quick to doubt!" a new voice said, and

they turned to see Lokane and four of his fighters coming up behind them. "Make it to the tunnels, then double back and head north so they can't find you. But, Rhona, for the love of the spirits, do not use your magic."

"Deal," she muttered, barely able to get the words out, and they ran. The sounds of fighting rose behind them as they reached the hillside below and disappeared into the darkness of the first tunnel entrance they came across.

CHAPTER TWELVE

Running through the dark tunnels again didn't exactly thrill Alastar, especially with the fact that they were all lacking energy after their narrow escape.

They had been at it for over an hour now, and each dark turn put him further on edge. Donnon's breathing came loud and raspy behind them, while Rhona stumbled on the verge of passing out.

"I—I need a minute," she said, pulling her arm free from his and leaning against the tunnel wall. She slid down it so that she could sit.

"They're back there, somewhere." Alastar nodded to Donnon whose relieved expression showed he was more than happy to join them. "If we stop now—"

"If we don't, we die," Rhona said. "If they were to catch us in this state, none of us could put up a fight."

Alastar leaned against the opposite wall, knowing she was right. They needed rest if they hoped to face whatever challenges awaited them.

He lowered his head and prayed for a blessing of

restoration, but only a soft glow covered them, barely noticeable. Still, Donnon let out a small gasp of relief, and Rhona's tired eyes looked slightly more awake—or maybe it was just the effect of the glow, highlighting her face.

When had she become so grownup? He couldn't believe that in the last day or so she had gone from his innocent, kind-hearted little sister to this woman who he felt he didn't really know anymore.

A thump sounded, echoing in the darkness beyond, back through the tunnels. Then a scurrying of feet, Alastar was certain. But as he held up a hand for silence and cocked his head to hear, no more sounds came.

Finally, he lowered his hand and shrugged.

"It's your nerves," Donnon said with a smile. "They'll get you every time."

Again, they sat in silence for a moment, until another sound startled Alastar. Only this time, it was coming from Rhona.

She was *laughing*.

"Are you… losing it?" he asked.

With a wave of her hand, she pushed herself up and let the laugh fade into a chuckle. "No, no, it's just… We were *amazing!*"

He just stared at her, then shook his head. "Yeah, you're gone. I've lost my sister to insanity."

"Not in the slightest." She held her hands in the air and said, "I'm loving it!"

"Can we keep our voices down?" Donnon pleaded with a nod back the way they had come.

"Bring 'em on. This place is all shadows, right? Imagine what I could do down here!"

"So, that's what it is then?" Alastar asked. "Your shadow magic, and me with my light."

"You admit it's magic?" Donnon stood now, too. "This denial thing is behind us?"

"First, it's not a 'denial thing,' it's my religion. Second, I'm not saying that what I do is magic. I was just pointing out that the blessing of Saint Rodrick clearly comes with a light element, while we're agreeing that Rhona's spells have a shadow element."

"It's pretty amazing," Rhona interjected. "I mean, imagine if we could figure out a way to not have the magic drain us… what we'd be capable of."

"Again, not we… I don't do magic."

"How can you still detest the idea of it, after everything?"

Alastar glared. "For all I know, you're in the process of turning evil, but just aren't there yet."

"Wait, what?"

"So, I'm evil, too?" Donnon asked, irritation heavy in his voice.

"I don't know!" Alastar shouted in frustration. "All I know is, my whole life I've been taught that magic is evil. Then suddenly, my sister can do it, and so I'm supposed to throw my beliefs into the embers and watch them burn?"

Rhona took a step over to Donnon's side, the two of them making a perfect pair with their protruding jaws and furrowed brows. So what if they didn't like what he had to say. It was the truth, and a paladin must always speak the truth.

"Since nothing found us after that yell," Donnon said,

finally breaking the silence, "I think that means we're in the clear, for now. It's best if we get some sleep."

Alastar opened his mouth to protest, but Rhona had nodded and started following Donnon to look for a place to lie down, so he figured he should keep his mouth shut for now. If there were any problems, they certainly would be better able to face them when rested.

When they were lying down in a side chamber, well hidden from the main tunnels by staggered walls, Alastar found a spot closest to the entrance and turned to the others.

"I'll take the first watch."

Rhona pursed her lips and said, "Don't trust me now that I'm one of them?"

"Them?"

"You know, an evil witch." Rhona smirked, but leaned back and let him take the watch.

Alastar stared after her and then made eye contact with Donnon before returning to his spot. He stared at the carved-out walls, contemplating this whole argument of good versus evil. What was evil, anyway? The Age of Madness had certainly brought a whole new kind of evil upon the world, one that hadn't existed before. How could it have? The entire world would have been consumed if that hadn't been put down. No one knew exactly what had happened. They knew that Saint Rodrick, though he hadn't been a saint at the time, had led the charge, securing old keeps and buildings from the time before for everyone to hunker down in. Then he had led a great charge against the men and women who had become monsters in the Age of Madness.

Out west, to Sair Talem.

If he had succeeded but fallen along the way, that's where his sword, the Sword of Light, would be. Everyone had thought him lost for some time. Then the Age of Madness had come to an end, and they all knew in their heart of hearts that it had been Rodrick's doing. He was named a saint, and the Order of Rodrick had been founded.

With so many years having passed between Rodrick setting off on his quest and the completion of the Age of Madness, could it be possible that he actually had nothing to do with it at all? That his sainthood was falsely awarded?

Such thoughts were strictly punished back under the rule of the High Paladin. Blasphemy, they would say. But now that Alastar was out here, giving his mind free reign, he had to wonder if it all didn't add up.

Even the argument about what he did, with the light and the blessings, made him wonder. If his blessings really were magic, then he was no better than all those men and women the Order of Rodrick had fought to persecute.

The idea that he had supported a system so wrong and corrupt made believing this could be possible incredibly difficult.

However, when he considered the fact that he, too, lost energy after a blessing, just like the others with their magic, he had to wonder.

He felt his head rolling and caught himself, eyes half-closed. Damn, he hadn't counted on being *this* tired. It was strange, he had to admit, how his healing could heal his physical body, but would always leave some amount of exhaustion behind. It was a different kind of exhaustion, too. His body and mind could be totally healthy and alert, while a part of him felt completely drained. His soul, maybe?

Again, his eyes closed. This time, he pushed himself up and shook out his limbs to get the blood flowing.

He yawned and turned back to the other two, then froze. Rhona slept beside Donnon, but had just rolled over and put her arm over his chest. Was it a conscious act? He couldn't be sure.

Cautiously, so as not to wake them, he tiptoed over and knelt beside the two, reaching out gingerly to lift her arm and put it back at her side.

A grunt came from her, and then she put her arm back around him and even cozied up to him this time.

Alastar frowned. He was about to intervene again when he looked up and saw Donnon's eyes open. The man took in the situation, saw Alastar kneeling there, and then smiled and raised an eyebrow. It was like he was daring Alastar to do something about it!

Frustration caused Alastar to instinctively clench his fists, but it wasn't like he could really start a fight over something his sister had started in her sleep. This guy was being an arse, but otherwise, he was likely to be their only help going forward.

So instead, Alastar said, "Your watch."

"So soon?" Donnon asked, but was already moving Rhona's arm and sitting up to take the watch.

As he went over to the entrance, Alastar said, "I'm watching you, just remember that."

"Odd, considering the fact that we're supposed to be watching for intruders."

"Maybe that's exactly what you are." The words came out before Alastar had time to think about them, but he stared, not backing down.

Donnon laughed with a shake of his head. "Your sister hasn't taken the same oaths you have, paladin. It would do her some good if you were to remember this."

"And you think she would settle for a clansman?"

"I think she'll do as she pleases, regardless of your own prejudices."

There wasn't much he could say to that, so Alastar took a spot beside his sister. He made sure he was far enough away that her arm couldn't find him if it had a life of its own, and then allowed his eyes to close.

While he hadn't ever really cared for the idea of romance, he found his sleep-filled mind fogging over with thoughts he had never had before. Whether she was joking or not, Estair had gotten under his skin with her comments. But it was more than that. She had also pulled at his interest with side glances, the hint of a smile, and simply the way she walked.

Everything within told Alastar to pay the price for these thoughts, to focus on his duty to the Order. The skin was a distraction, nothing more.

Well, everything except a very logical part of his brain that started as a hushed pulse somewhere in the darkness and grew louder and louder, and soon seemed to be screaming at him—*those days are gone!*

How could they really be, though? Duty and honor had always been a part of him, for as far back as he could remember. As he thought about it, his mind swirling with the night and pulling him out of consciousness, he considered that maybe his duty was just being redirected. Duty to the land, duty to its people.

Duty to his sister, and any magic user out there who might be wrongly accused.

He would put a stop to those sorcerers, as that was an immediate peril. And then? Well, then he would have to confront the Order of Rodrick and any others in the lowlands who held similar beliefs about magic users.

Then, and only then, he told himself, would he be allowed to consider a woman in the way he had been considering Estair.

With that thought, finally, sleep took him.

CHAPTER THIRTEEN

Rhona awoke to hushed whispers between the two men, but they stopped talking as soon as they noticed that she was awake. The first emotion she felt was annoyance that they had apparently let her sleep the longest and not given her a chance to stand watch. Second, in spite of the worry in Donnon's eyes, he seemed to have a hidden smile in there, as if he knew of some deep secret she didn't.

Her mind rushed back to the evening before, to falling asleep at his side, each sharing a comforting look and a nod that seemed to convey they both agreed that her brother could be a pain.

And yeah, she'd felt a flutter in her chest, but she hadn't told him about it or accepted the kiss she suspected he wanted to give her, based on the look in his eyes as they moved to her lips.

What had him all worked up?

She stood and smoothed out her clothes. The strong scent of sweat and dried blood was strong in the room, and her balance was off due to a slight ache in one ear. She reached up to smooth out her hair, only to find it in complete disarray.

"What is it?" she asked the two as she approached, blinking and doing her best not to wobble.

"Maybe nothing, maybe something," Donnon whispered.

"What Mr. Cryptic here means," Alastar said, also keeping his voice low, "is that we heard scuffling, like feet on dirt, and thought we might have even heard whispers."

"Maybe you need more sleep," she hissed, not addressing her comment specifically to either one of them.

Alastar shrugged, then motioned for silence with a finger to his lips.

Slightly annoyed that they couldn't address her complaints at the moment, but even more pissed at the fact that she wanted a nice bath and knew that she wasn't likely to get it in the near future, she closed her eyes to connect with the shadows.

There was indeed something out there.

"I sense them," she said, eyes still closed. It wasn't like she could see them, but she felt the shadows moving around her like a great lake of darkness. Something was definitely causing a ripple.

"How many?" Alastar asked.

"Not enough to piss your pants over," she replied, then opened her eyes to see him glaring. "Sorry, still waking up. I'm not used to this, so can't be sure. If I had to guess, I'd say a handful."

"Five or six we can take," Donnon said. "As long as they aren't the sorcerers, that is."

Alastar nodded and reached over to smooth out his sister's hair. "Let's get moving, but be at the ready."

She swatted his hand away, smoothed out her hair herself, and said, "I'm not sure how my appearance changes the fight at all."

"Actually…" Alastar pulled back, assessing her with a smirk. "We might want to keep the crazy witch look. Could scare them off."

"Personally, I like it," Donnon offered. "Makes you look…"

"Intimidating?" She teased her hair, so it stood out even more.

"I was going to say wild."

The look of annoyance that flashed across Alastar's face was hard to miss, but she ignored it. "Clansmen like their women wild, do they?"

"Aye. We want women that can keep up with us or lead the way. Not subservient cows like in the lowlands."

"Our women are not cows," Alastar said, his frustration growing.

"Clearly," Donnon replied with a wink Rhona's way.

She rolled her eyes, but couldn't help blushing. Hopefully, it wasn't noticeable in the dark tunnels.

"If this little flirt session is over, maybe we can get moving before whatever's out there catches us off-guard?" Alastar leaned out into the passage, glancing both ways, and then motioned for them to follow. "Quickly and quietly."

"I wouldn't know how to do either," Donnon said with a chuckle.

"You test me, warlock." Alastar turned, finger in the man's face. "Continue to do so, and we'll have a problem."

Donnon sneered as if he'd like to see that happen, but nodded and walked past Alastar, taking the lead.

"He's just having a bit of fun," Rhona hissed as she passed.

"That man has his eyes on you."

"And as I've said before, that's none of your business."

She could tell the words got to him, but that had been her intent. While he had helped raise her and had always been there for her, it was time he learned that she was a grown woman, even if just barely. She could make her own decisions, and accept a little flirting from an attractive man with a beard if she damn well pleased.

Plus, she found herself wondering about Donnon's comment now, and what it would actually be like to be with a clansman. Her whole life she had been told they were evil, capable of unspeakable things if they found a woman alone at night. Donnon didn't seem so bad, and definitely didn't live up to the horror stories. She wondered if his beard would tickle her inner thighs, and what his gruff voice would sound like when he moaned.

Her one experience with a man had been quite the odd one, she thought as the three made their way down dark tunnels, only lit by a faint glow from her brother. One night in the castle, she had been finishing her bath when Sir Taland had entered. He wasn't supposed to be in the women's bathing chambers, but he stood there, leaning against the doorway, simply watching her.

At the time, she had been more curious than offended, and had simply turned and stood, facing him as the water dripped from her nude form. He had licked his lips and brushed his long, blond hair behind his ear as he approached, then guided her to sit at the edge of the bath. Before she knew it, he was kneeling before her, and his tongue was giving her unknown pleasures.

It had been a brief encounter, one she had never experienced before nor since, and never discussed with anyone. When it was over, he had simply turned away, ashamed, and asked that she never let word of that escape, or he would lose his seat as a paladin.

How many nights had she lain awake in her night robes, staring at the door and wondering, no, hoping he would return?

But it never happened again, and he purposefully avoided her gaze at all dinners and elsewhere.

Now, she found those same urges returning as she watched the dark form of Donnon walking ahead. His broad shoulders took up most of the hall, and she wondered if, somehow the two of them were ever to be interlocked in ecstasy, would their magic burst forth as they lost control?

It was almost a humorous thought, and she couldn't help but snicker silently. Apparently, Donnon heard because he slowed enough to glance back at her with a raised eyebrow.

"Everything good?" he asked.

She just bit her lip and walked past him, taking the lead. Instantly, she regretted the action, because now she kept imagining he was staring at her rear as she walked.

Then again, maybe that wasn't such a bad thing.

A swoosh sounded, and the shadows seemed to sway in

warning, a subconscious call upon her magic, she imagined, and ducked. With a clatter, an arrow hit the wall nearby.

"There!" she said, pointing in the direction it had come from.

Before either of the others could react, a piercing shout rang through the tunnels, and a second later a spear glinted in Alastar's glow. Donnon appeared, knocking the spear aside and then kicking at a remnant's knee so that it busted. He spun and elbowed the remnant in the head before wrapping his arm around its neck and throwing it over his hip. When it thudded to the ground, he was quick to maneuver around it and snap the bastard's neck.

Alastar's sword clanged against that of another, and then two more remnant were on top of them as Donnon snatched up the spear and joined the fight to push them back.

While Alastar was fast with his sword, more than once the tight confines of the tunnel worked against him.

One of the remnant nearly landed a blow to his head with its battleax, but Donnon was at his side a moment later, skewering the remnant and snatching the ax out of the air as it fell.

"Now, this is more like it!" he bellowed, and turned back to press the attack.

Rhona closed her eyes, considering the risk of letting the darkness in, letting it carry her forward to join in the fight.

She opened her eyes to see Alastar there, shaking his head.

"Save your energy, we've got this."

He turned to join the fight and, sure enough, within seconds they had taken out the remnant, and the way was clear.

Their heavy breathing filled the darkness and Alastar turned with a smile. Except, another ripple came from the shadows. Something moving away, and fast.

"A scout," she said, pointing. "He's gone to warn the others."

"Well, spirits curse them!" Donnon shouted, tightly gripping his new ax and preparing to run.

Alastar held up a hand, stopping him, and then motioned to Rhona. "Now would be an okay time to pull on those powers of yours… if you think you can handle it?"

Her chest felt heavy with worry, but she closed her eyes and focused.

The ripples became a wave, and then it was like she was at one with the shadows. A form was moving, his breaths raspy and heavy, his stench thick and putrid, so that when she engulfed him, and he fell to the floor, suffocating, it was almost too much for her to keep the connection. Shadows twisted and turned around the man, pressing in on him. Then, with a shout mixed with anger and excitement, she pushed so that the shadows simply took him.

He was gone.

She returned to see her brother and stumbled, but it was Donnon who caught her.

"Is he…?"

She blinked, trying to figure out what had just happened, but then nodded. "Gone." Donnon's arms felt comforting, and she was glad he didn't let go, as her head was spinning.

Still, she found herself feeling better quickly, and wondered if maybe focusing her energy on one person like that instead of multiple took less out of her. Alastar held up his hands and looked about to pray for a blessing of healing, but she shook her head. "Save your energy."

He was surprised, but nodded and was about to lead the way onwards when he looked back at Donnon and frowned.

"Right," Donnon said with a laugh as he stepped back, and only then did Rhona realize that the man still had his arm around her. "Just being cautious."

"Sure you are." Alastar took off without another look back.

Rhona followed close behind, not wanting Donnon to see her smile. If she was being honest with herself, she liked the attention. That didn't mean she needed to let him know that.

While she was admitting stuff to herself, she realized she actually liked this shadow magic. This power was unlike anything she had ever felt in life. So many days growing up had been spent looking out from the castle ramparts at the paladins training below, admiring the blessings they were able to pull down with their so-called prayers.

Now she knew that it had all just been magic, even if her brother wasn't ready to admit it. His light magic combined with her shadow magic. It got her thinking, wondering how powerful the two could be if they set their minds to it—well, if Alastar ever accepted his powers for what they were.

A howl sounded in the tunnels behind them, and

Alastar turned, casting a soft glow back that way. His sword lit up as he prayed, and he said, "More scouts, likely. They won't know which way we went, so we might luck out. But we'd best hurry."

Seeing by the light of his sword, they darted past old, crumbling roads that lead through tunnels and various buried parts of old cities. Each time they exited one tunnel, they'd breathe fresh air, happy to be out on green hills, only to return to a new set of tunnels shortly after.

The shouting had died down, and they had just emerged onto a plateau that led to a series of lakes and rivers past the valley ahead, when Donnon pointed and swore.

Rhona didn't need to ask why, as she too saw the plumes of smoke rising from amongst a clump of trees in the distance.

"I take it you know what's burning over there?" Alastar said.

"If the terror in my gut is correct, aye." Donnon rested the ax on his shoulder and turned, looking for any sign of danger. "That's where my village is."

Alastar didn't say another word, but simply nodded and pressed on. Rhona's legs were killing her, and her stomach ached from hunger, but she kept moving. His little girl, Kia… If she was hurt in any way, Donnon would most assuredly lose it. She understood how important this was for him, but wondered what dangers might await them below.

CHAPTER FOURTEEN

Donnon cared for nothing more at that moment than his little girl and her safety. Leaving her with just two of his friends while she had the black marks of the plague on her had been risky. Stupid even. He had put everything he had into his decision to go find a healer, and he had found one.

But now this? To return with Alastar and his healing magic, only to find his village in flames was more than he could bear.

He was vaguely aware of the other two racing along with him, of plowing their way down through the valley and then following it up through dew-covered bushes to the point that led up and toward his village. Part of him knew it was gone, everything would be gone, but he couldn't give up hope yet.

They passed the river he'd often taken Kia to when teaching her to swim, and the rock he would always remember where he had once slipped, almost lost control, and then dropped his daughter. He had never taken her to the river again after that, afraid he might lose her, too, after the illness that had taken her mother from them.

Smoke rose in thin tendrils past the trees ahead, not much now. That told him the fire was at its end, and that it would have claimed its prize long before he arrived.

The worst part was that, had he been there, he would have been able to control the flames, to put a stop to this. Had any of the fire mages been there, his daughter would still be alive. They had abandoned him in his time of need, and he'd have words with them yet.

But for now, he needed to block the negativity out, keep focused, and be certain of what had happened here. Hope burned in his gut, as slight as that ball of hope was, yearning for the off-chance that his daughter was still alive.

Then he was running through trees, and the first burnt house lay in ashes before him. Past it were more, and then he was among it all, collapsing to his knees, staring in horror.

"Kia…" It was barely a whisper. It was all gone. They… they were all gone. "Kia!" Donnon pushed himself up, refusing to believe it, and spun around, looking for any other way they might have survived, any sign of who might have done this.

"Donnon," Rhona said, arriving at the edge of the clearing, her hand clasped to her heart, the other at her mouth. "Oh, my… I'm so sorry."

"KIA!" he shouted again, refusing to accept that she could be gone. Not his little girl.

"It's too late," Alastar said, looking at the carnage. He walked over and put a hand on Donnon's shoulder.

Donnon's first instinct was to swat the hand aside, to

punch the man for even thinking Kia could be dead, but instead he bit his lip and let the sorrow ball up in anger. Whoever had done this would pay, whoever was responsible would—

"Father...?" a voice said, and he turned, warmth spreading throughout his body as that hope, the hope that had nearly been quenched, exploded.

There she was, still covered in the black marks, but beautiful as ever. He was kneeling in front of her in an instant, wrapping her in his arms, caressing her hair, and weeping.

"My baby, my amazing Kia." He pulled back, looking for her protectors.

But she shook her head, her hazel eyes full of sorrow.

"They're gone," he said in realization.

"They tried to fight," Kia said. "They took me to the caves and then led a distraction, but... never made it back."

He knew how hard that must have been for her, so he pulled her back in for a hug. No more questions, not now.

When she coughed, he remembered the two he had brought, and quickly stood, gesturing to Alastar.

"This is her, my Kia," he said, pride welling up inside as Alastar's eyes went wide at the sight of her. "My little survivor."

"It's a pleasure to meet you," Alastar said, assessing her disease. "Would you be okay with me trying something?"

She stared up at him, her nine-year-old trust uncertain in this condition, what with all she had been through. Finally, she nodded. Donnon couldn't imagine leaving her side in a moment like this, so he held her tight as Alastar stepped up and placed his hand on her forehead. The paladin's eyes closed, and his lips moved in prayer, and soon a bright light moved down his arm and swept over her until her entire body glowed golden.

He opened his eyes, and they were gold as well, and he said, "By the Order of Rodrick and the blessing of the holy saint, be healed, child."

The light engulfed her even as she stepped back and whimpered in terror, pulling away from him and even her own father's grip. Her arms flailed as she tried to fight off the light, screaming, "No, not you, no! No!"

Donnon couldn't understand what was happening, so at first, he turned to Alastar, ax raised, but he looked as dumbfounded as Donnon felt.

Instead, he dropped the ax and ran to his daughter, holding her by the shoulders as he begged her to tell him what was wrong.

"Him!" she shouted, pointing at Alastar even as the light faded, taking the black marks with it. "He's one of them! He's one of them!"

Donnon was still lost, but Rhona was at his side a moment later, one arm on his shoulder, the other on his daughter's.

"I think I understand," Rhona said, clearly trying to convey calmness. "His prayer, the Order of Rodrick…"

Kia flinched at the name.

"You called?" a new voice said, and they all turned to see a dozen paladins. At their head was a tall knight with long, golden hair shining in the sun almost as brightly as his white and gold armor. His eyes took them in with malice at first, until they came to rest on Rhona and Alastar. He frowned in confusion, then smiled. "It seems you've lost your armor, brother."

"Taland…" Alastar stood, hand on the hilt of his sword. "Did you do this?"

"Our war is with these witches and warlocks," Taland said. "Or did you forget what they did to our castle?" His eyes moved back to Rhona, and there was something else there. Shame? Spite?

Alastar shook his head. "The sorcerers who attacked the castle had nothing to do with these people."

"They all use magic, they are all evil. What else is there to know?"

"You don't understand, brothers." Alastar motioned to Kia. "You would wage war on a child over this?"

"Her?" Taland laughed, and the others snickered. "Her most of all. Who do you think burned the village down while we sought shelter?"

Donnon turned to his daughter, confused. She had never shown her magic to others, but now he saw it there in her eyes—confidence, a burning hatred, and power. She wasn't hiding anymore.

He had hoped she wouldn't be burdened with this power, at times a curse, at others a blessing.

At the moment, it was clearly bound to be the latter. He pulled out his flint and prepared to light it, when an armored kick hit him in the ribs, knocking the flint out of his hands. He lunged to reach for it, when another paladin stomped on his hand, and the cracking of bones sent a piercing pain up Donnon's arm.

"Stop it!" Kia screamed, running for them, but Rhona held her back.

"Your war is not with them!" Rhona shouted.

Taland stepped up to her, furious, and raised his hand to strike, but it never came. Instead, he had been distracted by something beyond her.

Now, Donnon and the others turned to look too. All around them, Remnant were emerging through the trees. Hundreds of them.

"The hell is this sorcery?" Taland asked, lowering his hand to draw his sword. "You… you all control them somehow? You called them here?"

"You poor, ignorant *arse*." Donnon cradled his injured hand and scooted over to his daughter. "I hope they don't kill you, so that I'll have the chance one day."

Taland didn't seem to like that remark much, because he brought the hilt of his sword down on Donnon's head with a strike that sent him spinning down into darkness.

CHAPTER FIFTEEN

Alastar stared in shock as Donnon crumbled to the ground, unconscious, and his daughter screamed and lunged for him. The remnant were everywhere, and now there was this to deal with.

If this had been anyone other than Taland, he wouldn't have worried, but Taland had been one of the few paladins who had often bested him both in sparring and blessings.

As the other paladins all called down blessings upon themselves, and their bodies and swords glowed, Alastar tried to lift his sword and found the spell to heal Kia had taken too much from him.

He staggered over to Rhona's side, but before he could make it, Taland had given an order and three of the paladins had taken hold of him and were dragging him away, while the others formed a defensive retreat formation.

"There's too many," Taland said, and then pointed at Kia. "Kill them first, including the sister."

"No!" Alastar shouted, trying to fight, trying to call

down a blessing, but he couldn't. He was simply too drained.

The paladins moved for them, but Rhona was over by the other two, grabbing them, and she cast a look back at Alastar as she mouthed, "I'll find you," and then all three had become shadow, darting away.

He leaned back, letting the paladins take him as he sighed in relief.

A crack in the sky startled him, and he lifted his head to see that, to his dismay, three shadowy forms were falling from the sky. They fell toward a glowing, purple mist that circled beneath, and then the mist had them.

For a moment, Alastar was certain he saw a face in that mist—the chief sorcerer who he had seen at the fortress and then again in the pursuit. Irdin, they'd called him.

The bastard had them, and there was nothing Alastar could do about it. He thrashed and shouted, but the paladins had him and, as they were strengthened by the blessings, he was like a child struggling against several grown men.

"They have her!" he shouted. "The sorcerers, that's what they wanted. Her!"

"We'll have words with the sorcerers," Taland assured him, marching past as his men met the first of the remnant with a clash of swords against whatever crude axes and hammers they had. "But your sister and the other two? We don't give a damn."

Warfare sounded nearby, and Alastar was tossed to the ground with a thud as his captors turned to slay nearby remnant. He had never felt so powerless as at that moment, and hoped it hadn't all been for nothing. Had he healed that little girl only to watch her die at the hands of the sorcerers?

These were his brothers in arms, more than family at one time, now tossing him about like a mere prisoner. How quickly one could turn from trusted friend to enemy. He lay there, watching blood fly from those creatures that were clearly once human but now survived in a feral state of perpetual anger and bloodlust. Maybe they, too, were somehow simply misunderstood.

Had anyone ever captured one and sat down to try and converse with it? Or even better, tried to heal one?

Not that any of that much mattered. Either the remnant would somehow overpower the paladins, the sorcerers would join up with them for the attack, or they would escape and either kill him for his betrayal or make an example out of him in some other way.

Those weren't scenarios he was prepared to let happen.

An opening appeared, and he stood, making ready to run for it, only to find an armored, glowing arm clothes-line him and send him flying back to the ground with a hard thump on his back.

He gasped for air and stared up at another face he recognized, Sir Bale, shaking his head and shouting something about staying down.

Forget that.

Again, he pushed himself up, this time finding a bit of prayer led to a response. His skin tingled and filled with energy, and then he was up, pushing past Bale and going for his sword where it lay on the ground.

Two remnant charged him, and he caught the first one with an uppercut, but felt the other's club against his side with a pain that shook his insides. He lifted his fist to strike, when a strange sensation came over him. A bright light flashed before his eyes, blinding him, and he guessed the same had happened to the remnant, because they all screamed at once.

He was swinging wildly, only able to see faint outlines around him. Something swooshed past his face, then a form appeared and had him. More hands grabbed him, and they lifted him off of the ground, carrying him away from that place.

"We've got you," Bale said. "Don't worry, you're safe... for now."

Alastar stopped struggling long enough to ask, "And the others? The sorcerers?"

"After they got what they came for, they were gone."

It took a moment to process this. Had the sorcerers really been after his sister? He couldn't figure out why, except for her unique magic. Magic the likes of which he had never heard of anyone else using before.

All of this had started because he had to be the hero back in that farm house. He wished he had a magic that he could use to go back and change that moment, although he had to admit that, if she had the power in her laying dormant, it likely would have come out eventually anyway.

Soon, his captors let his feet fall to the ground, and he was being half-dragged as he ran along with them, and then gradually his sight began to slowly recover enough to where he could make out colors.

This might mean the powers of their blessings were weakening, giving him hope once more.

"The sorcerers who attacked," he said as they stumbled on, "we have to warn the High Paladin."

"Sir Gildon knows who his enemies are," Bale's voice came from his side. "As of right now, you happen to be one of them. So, don't be looking our way for help."

Alastar gritted his teeth, processing the information that Sir Gildon had survived the attack on the castle, but had it out for him. After a few more steps and as his vision cleared further, he added, "We all saw it. They were performing magic unlike anything we've experienced before. They're not the clansmen, I promise you."

"And I promise you no one gives a rat's arse," another voice said, one he couldn't quite place. "Sir Gildon has ordered that you serve as an example for what happens when paladins betray their kind in favor of the dark arts."

So that's how it was. He wasn't just being dragged off randomly, but to be crucified for the others to see, so that none would make his mistake. His broken body would be a lesson for all.

If that was the case, he was determined to find a way out of this before that could happen. It also meant there was no way these so-called brothers would help him rescue Rhona and the others.

Somehow, he would have to break free, and he would have to do it on his own.

CHAPTER SIXTEEN

Rhona had felt like her soul was being pulled out in every direction, and the next thing she knew she, Donnon, and Kia were falling from the sky. They had been engulfed by purple clouds of the sorcerer, though she didn't truly see him until she had hit the ground.

When he had approached, all she could manage was a croak of, "Stay back."

The man who had last spoken to her when she was still back with Estair, the same who had attacked the Castle of the Order of Rodrick, stood before her now. His eyes began to fade from full black to a sharp blue, and the magic around them faded.

He smiled, and she was aware of the sounds of battle not far off. The paladins and the remnant, she imagined.

"Since you already had your chance to join us," Master Irdin said, "I'm sorry to say this round won't be so hospitable." He nodded to his right, where the man with blond hair and white eyes appeared. "Instead, we'll simply have to take over that brain of yours."

The thought of this freak of a mystic entering her mind made her stomach churn.

She turned, looking for an escape route, and then realized there wasn't much room for physical escape when the attack is coming on a mental plane. She saw Donnon there on the ground nearby, pulling himself over to his daughter.

If Kia was hurt, or dead, these sorcerers would feel no end to the wrath of Rhona.

She sighed a breath of relief when she saw Kia reach out and take her father's hand. Donnon helped his daughter to sit, and then cradled her in his arms, and she wrapped him in hers.

The sight sent a warmth through Rhona that pushed aside all pain and doubt, and she turned to the mystic and smiled.

"Let's see what you've got," she said, and then felt her eyes cloud over as she saw his turn white.

She knew she couldn't fight the evil mystic's magic with simply the power of her mind, as he was too skilled and powerful for that. So instead, she presented him with a new type of challenge. When he attempted to enter her mind, she was ready for him—she let the shadow in, knowing that all he would find was darkness.

His presence tingled, letting her know he was in there, and she pushed in on him at every angle. If he couldn't get a read on her, he couldn't do any damage.

Next, she focused on the darkness, letting herself fall into it, and then embracing it so that it was everything.

With a shout of frustration, Wodain stepped back, holding his head, and tears of black fell down his cheeks.

"That witch!" he shouted, pulling up his red shirt to

reveal long black lines on his skin, moving like internal snakes. "Look what she's done to me!"

Even she didn't know what she had done, but she wouldn't give him the satisfaction of knowing that, so she stared him in the eyes and said, "See what happens if you try again."

"This isn't working," Master Irdin said, standing over her, his eyes weighing her. "Wodain, you've failed."

"Excuse me?" the mystic asked.

"When we return to *Her*, she shall know of your failure." He frowned at Rhona, then the other two. "This is *sickening*."

"And you'd be any farther along without me?" Wodain cocked his head. Eyes turning white.

"Stay out of my mind, child," Master Irdin said, turning on his companion. "Or I'll remind you why She named me head of this campaign. It won't be a pleasant reminder."

Rhona watched all of this, intrigued. Infighting was always good, when it was amongst the opposing side.

As they continued their bickering, she glanced back to see Donnon and Kia whispering, but gave them a stern glance and a nod of her head toward Wodain. If he could read minds, planning an escape wasn't likely to work. However, he was distracted, and if she could keep that distraction going, it just might work.

She held up a finger to signify for them to wait a moment, and then turned back to Wodain and, instead of simply releasing her powers, she focused. She had no idea what she was doing, really, but she imagined his mind and focused on the shadows, almost like she was pushing on his brain.

His voice rose as he said, "She would cower before me if she knew what I was truly capable of." He spun on Master Irdin, hand held out as if he expected the man's heart to fall into it.

"AHHH!" Master Irdin shouted, grabbing his head. He spun, moving his hands in motion before his chest and then pushed out with fingers extended. The air surrounding them grew cold and Wodain was wrapped up in a whirlwind of snow and ice that suddenly froze, holding him in midair as if time had stopped.

"Don't let them into your head!" Master Irdin commanded, and then spun on Rhona, pointing so that one of the spears of ice redirected and shot at her, stopping an inch from her throat.

It was so close, she could feel the cold from it.

"And you," he said, "don't go about thinking you're invincible."

"Do it then!"

His eyes burned with hatred, and his hand shook. "You are valuable to a certain someone, but you try something like that again… just remember that I can cause a lot of pain without killing you."

With a wave, he released the spell that held Wodain. The mystic fell to the ground with a grunt.

"What the hell happened?" Wodain asked, pushing himself up. When his eyes moved to Rhona, they went wide. "That little birdy… how?"

"Just focus on keeping the remnant in line," Master Irdin said, then raised a fist as if signaling someone. Sure enough, a light appeared in the sky, growing close. He stared at Rhona, moving his jaw as if he wanted to bite her head off. "I'm going to assume you're drained after that little stunt. How convenient for us."

With a flash of light, the other two sorcerers who had been with him appeared, one on each side of Rhona as they dragged her off.

"No, Rhona!" Donnon said, standing, ready to pursue.

One glance from Wodain's white eyes sent him to the ground, screaming. Kia collapsed over him, screaming for Wodain to stop, but Rhona didn't see what happened next, because the two sorcerers had pulled her forward and over the crest of a hill.

Master Irdin paused, then went back. He followed a moment later with Kia kicking and screaming in his clutches, then tossed her at one of the other sorcerer's feet.

"Why?"

"So you don't try anything stupid," he replied, and joined her to look back over the remnant. They seemed to be staggering about in confusion, some regaining their focus now that Wodain was putting his spell back on them.

A distant look came over Master Irdin's eyes, and his hand went out as if to grab hold of something. A weapon, maybe? Then Rhona realized it wasn't a weapon he was reaching for at all, but something to balance on.

He was weak!

"So, you're like the rest of us after all," she said.

"I'm nothing like you," he said, regaining his composure. "For one, I will live beyond tomorrow. You? You'll have your brain harvested, your magic learned, and then your vegetable of a body tossed to the remnant for feeding."

There was no way to digest that idea, she thought with

a gulp. But instead of showing him her fear, she forced a laugh and said, "Then what the *hell* are we waiting for?"

"You're new to this whole magic thing, so I'll ignore your ignorance—this time. We just teleported here. When magic is used, especially such magic for long distances and based on hearsay, a bit of a recovery time is required."

She turned back toward the trees that now blocked her view of the area where they had left Donnon. He had come all this way to find a healer, and succeeded, only to end up like this.

"The man, did you… kill him?"

Master Irdin raised an eyebrow. "He meant something to you? Well, I hope it was purely physical, because his mind will be no better than a remnant if he survives what Wodain sent his way."

"You're a monster," Rhona spat.

"I'm a product of my upbringing, as are you. The difference is that I'm a survivor and a conqueror. You? You're simply a means to an end."

"Yes, your end."

He laughed. "Unfortunately for you, child, I'm destined for greatness. Divinity, as a matter of fact. So, tell me… how many gods have you slain?"

"Any world that would allow you to become a god would be one I'd happily leave behind, and anyone willing to worship you would deserve that poor excuse for a world."

His smile faded and his brow furrowed as he assessed her. "Troth, please remember that the girl dies if this one tries anything. I'll be resting." With that, he walked off to disappear behind a rock formation with gnarled trees growing out of it.

Rhona looked at Troth and then Wodain, wondering if she'd be able to make a move before those two were able to stop her. Or more importantly, before they were able to hurt Kia.

She couldn't take the risk, so instead, she sat down, cross-legged, and closed her eyes. When the moment was right, she wanted to ensure she had every ounce of strength she could possibly muster, and that meant resting right now.

She awoke as a shadow fell over her, and she looked up to see Master Irdin, his gray robes flapping in the wind.

"It's time," he said, and then formed a square with his fingers, which he extended and then twisted so that a gushing of wind sounded around them and then suddenly, their surroundings were gone.

She blinked, confused by the purple glow that lit an otherwise dark, great hall.

"Welcome to my home," Master Irdin said, stepping forward to reveal Kia nearby. "The two of you can get better acquainted. We'll need you close, after all, if we're going to bet on you not wanting to see her killed so that you can give us your mind and powers."

"That'll never happen," Rhona said.

Master Irdin stared with his icy glare. "When She arrives, we shall see."

His robes flowed as he spun and walked up the nearby stairs to join his companions. They all left, leaving Rhona and Kia alone in the room. Now that he was gone, it was clear this was some sort of dungeon. They weren't constrained, but judging by the clicks and clanks on the door after the others exited, they were locked down here.

Kia looked up at Rhona, eyes wide with fright. "You were with my father?"

The words didn't come, so instead Rhona nodded and held out her arms. Kia ran to her, accepting the embrace, and the two stood there like this for a few minutes.

Finally, Rhona said, "Don't worry, child. I'm going to get us out of here. You see, this place is full of shadows, and shadows are my friend."

Kia looked up at her, hopeful, and then smiled. "I can manipulate fire."

"Can you?"

Kia nodded.

"Well then, it looks like we're well on track to finding your father. Let's make every step count."

CHAPTER SEVENTEEN

When Alastar found himself tied to a tree and noticed the others putting up camp, he knew they were out of the immediate danger. They, but not him.

His first thought was to pray for a blessing of strength, but when he tried, nothing happened. He clenched his fists, eyes closed as he focused, but it was no use. His faith was at its lowest. And how could it not be, with the conflicting emotions about the war on magic, and his former brothers in arms turning on him?

But most of all, he was discouraged by the fact that he had been unable to stop the sorcerers from taking his sister. He had seen her fend for herself, but he had just healed Kia. How long would it take the girl to regenerate her powers without his healing to assist her along the way?

Taland approached and stood over him, sneering.

"You're making a mistake here," Alastar grumbled. "We have no idea what we're dealing with."

"Perhaps you don't, as you've lost your way." Taland sneered. "But we do. It's evil, plain and simple."

"The only thing plain or simple about this whole situation is you, if you think that's the truth."

Taland's jaw jutted out, but then he flipped his hair back and laughed. "Oh, I've missed you, Alastar. You know, none of the other paladins could ever even hope to stand a chance against me when it came to sword play. But you? You made it fun."

"This isn't a game, Taland."

"Isn't it, though?" He shifted on his feet so that the sunlight glinted off of his armor. "The dance we all dance. Temptations, little harlots like your sister weaving their magic in the world until we bring them down… All of it. And I've won."

"Leave my sister out of it, or I'll tear out that tongue of yours and use it to wipe my arse, you piece of shite."

"Whoa, the language on you since going rogue." Taland's eyes narrowed as he glanced around to ensure no one was listening. "Did I ever tell you about the time she tried to seduce me?"

Alastar struggled, snarling, but the ropes were too well secured.

"It's true," Taland continued, "one day when she was bathing, and I happened to be passing. She called me in and presented herself to me, as naked as the day she was born. It was a sight, let me tell you. The most perfect, perky little breasts you've ever seen. Naturally, I turned her away out of disgust—disgust that she would attempt to sway one of the holy knights of the Order of Rodrick. But she pleaded, can you imagine that? She ran at me from the bath, water dripping down her body like tiny fingers caressing her every inch, and knelt before me, begging that you would never find out from me."

"Let me guess, you made her that promise."

"After she… earned it." Taland's eyes sparkled with spite-filled humor.

"Two problems with that story," Alastar said, focusing on controlling his temper. "First, I don't believe she'd ever stoop to your level. Second, if that's true, that means you just broke your promise. So, either you lied about the story, or broke your promise to her, meaning that either way you're immoral. You don't deserve the armor you wear."

"At least I still wear my armor," Taland growled, then punched Alastar across the jaw with his gauntleted hand. The blow caused a sharp pain and ringing in Alastar's ears, bringing back memories of a similar time when he'd lost in the sparring ring and yielded, but still been struck by this same guy. He should have known at that moment that Taland wasn't pure of heart.

And now that he tasted blood, he thought back to other moments in his upbringing. The time when two women had left Sir Gildon's chambers, blushing. He had never even considered what possibly could have been going on in there. When the servants had gossiped about strange chanting in the night, and Alastar had been tasked with shutting them up. Or the time he had walked past the baths to find his sister join him, still damp, and give Taland a slight, secretive smile.

Had it all been a lie?

Taland was laughing, but it seemed so distant at that moment. Everything Alastar had dismissed as ridiculous came flooding back into his memory at that moment, and he found himself questioning everything he knew about the Order of Rodrick.

And if the Order could be doubted, maybe all of this talk of the prayers actually being magic were true, too?

He didn't need faith or prayers, in that case. All he would need was a belief that he could call upon this energy, whatever it was, and make the spells happen. Right?

A light appeared before his eyes, and for a moment, he thought he was simply seeing spots due to the hit he'd taken. But then he saw it had a shape like a human and was nodding its head.

Wait, was this thing telling him he was right? Answering his internal thought?

He forced his eyes wide, blinking, and saw that it was certainly not an illusion. There was a spirit of light, like a little angel, or maybe a fairy, hovering in the air inches in front of his eyes.

"What sorcery is this?" Taland demanded, and a moment later Bale and two others ran up, but froze in their tracks.

"He's one of 'em," Bale said in a mixture of awe and betrayal. "Alastar's turned warlock on us."

"Wrong," Alastar whispered, eyes focused on the little fairy. "I've seen the light, and it's glorious."

As his eyes shone, the fairy darted around and zipped through the ropes that bound him, thus setting him free. Others drew swords while he held out his hand for the fairy to alight on.

If what he understood about the clansmen was true, based on what the visiting mystics Volney and Larick had said, this was more of a manifestation of his magic. A way for his mind to cope with it, and to harness the spells.

Very well. It was time to get to harnessing.

With a flick of his wrist, the spirit transformed into a bright light and then exploded outward into intense beams of light that burned through even the paladins' armor.

None dropped dead, but all were felled by the intense pain. They writhed on the ground as the glowing beams became light snakes that slithered across their bodies, causing spasms of more pain with each second.

Alastar walked among them, only pausing to take Taland's sword and stomp on the man's outstretched hand. When he was at the edge of their group, he called back the spirit and said, "Find them."

It nodded again, and then zipped away. He stood for a moment, unsure what to do, and then sprinted after it to the calls of revenge from his former brothers behind him.

He was done with his old ways. Now, he would be a new sort of paladin, one that fought for justice and honor, not for some forced beliefs filled with hypocrisy and lies. Now, he would fight for his sister, Donnon, and little Kia. He would fight to ensure their safety, and he would oppose all who stood in the path of righteousness.

The way ahead was littered with remnant, and the spirit of light was leading him right toward a cluster of them. They seemed to be gathering around something, or someone, writhing on the ground.

A group saw him and charged, but he quickly learned why Taland had bested him so many times in the training grounds of the castle—this sword was lighter, easier to maneuver, and seemed to have an extra boost to each swing. That, or this light surrounding him was giving him more strength than he had ever experienced.

He sliced through three of them, their wild eyes sure to cause him nightmares. An ax came from a fourth, which he dodged. Weaving around the creature, he came up with a thrust that impaled two more of them. Kicking them off of his sword, he lifted one and used it as a shield to charge through the rest to reach the light fairy.

As he burst through the crowd of remnant, he tossed the body aside and then froze. Before him was Donnon, just now pushing himself to his feet. The man's clothes were singed, a circle of still smoldering remnant bodies surrounding him.

"Donnon?"

The others looked between the two of them, unsure what to do.

Donnon didn't seem to process what was going on, his eyes looking crazed as he spun, searching for something. His eyes landed on Alastar, but didn't recognize him, and he lunged forward with fists flailing. With the light-fueled energy, Alastar had no trouble dodging, but the circle of remnant forming around them was a problem. Since he had given up his armor before leaving the Fortress of Stirling, he kept having to watch his back for their spear thrusts and hatchet chops.

"Donnon, it's me!" he shouted while slapping a punch aside and back stepping, "Snap out of it!"

All he got was a grunt in return, and a lunge that caught him off-guard. No strike came, but Donnon's teeth came for Alastar's throat. He barely had time to catch the man, but then, just as he was struggling to keep the freakishly strong clansman from tearing out his larynx with his teeth, Alastar had a thought—this man wasn't in his right mind, and maybe he could heal his mind? It was a better plan than killing him.

Instead of fighting him, Alastar grabbed hold of Donnon and turned his head just enough to avoid getting bitten. He had never healed without a prayer before, but the action came like second nature. Gold glowed in his eyes, and he smiled as the energy seeped out of him and into Donnon.

One moment Donnon craved blood and only saw a monster before him—a man who would do anything to hurt him and everything he cared about in the world, though he himself wasn't sure what that meant. All he cared about was inflicting pain.

The next moment, he was in the man's arms, warmth coming over him like a soothing bath on a cool day mixed with a pleasant spring breeze. All of his senses came streaming back, and a fog cleared from his mind.

When the man released him, he staggered away and looked up to see a weathered Alastar, smiling back at him.

He was about to return the smile when he noticed the army of remnant that had formed a circle around them.

"We did it," Alastar said, stumbling to one knee. He pushed himself back up, glanced around and said, "Now, we'd better run like hell."

All Donnon could do was mutter, "What?"

"They… they have Kia."

At those words, a new power rose within Donnon as he remembered his little girl's face as she had healed earlier that day. All concept of time had faded, judging by the position of the sun in the sky, it couldn't have been *that* long ago.

The closest remnant paused long enough for them to see skin that looked to be rotting, and this one was taller than the rest, eyes dark. He sniffed, then snarled. "Let's kill these bastards," it said in a gravelly voice, then charged.

"NOW!" Alastar shouted, and tossed Donnon his sword.

Donnon caught it and tested its balance before spinning and chopping off the top half of the remnant's head. It went spinning through the air and slapped another in the face.

Then, all hell broke loose.

Luckily for Donnon, he was full of energy, and his mind was at its peak—he saw that the fallen remnant wore a crude metal breastplate, so he quickly struck the sword against it and watched with excitement as a spark formed. He did it again, and this time pulled from his internal energy, unleashing the potential of that spark so that it shot forward, creating a path through the remnant.

"On me!" he called back to Alastar, and together the two darted past the burnt grass and flaming bodies of remnant that had been caught in the fire.

He was almost past the small army before they even began to realize what was happening, but when he glanced over his shoulder, he saw that Alastar was lagging.

Dammit, he must've used his magic to heal him, which meant he couldn't very well be left behind.

Giving it his all, Donnon began to cut down remnant

left and right. One leaped over the others and almost had him, but Donnon thrust the sword up and skewered it in the air, continuing the trajectory so that the remnant flew off of the sword and knocked over two more.

"I can manage," Alastar said, holding his hand up to cast a ball of light as he caught up. "Close your eyes."

Even behind closed eyelids, the flash was bright. When Donnon looked again, the nearby remnant were blinking. One swung wildly, taking down another at its side.

Alastar wrapped an arm around Donnon and said, "Get me to safety, and we'll find your daughter and my sister."

"Deal," Donnon replied, and the two took off in a staggering run.

The remnant were fast, but each time one caught up with them, Donnon would drop it with a swipe of the sword. One tried to throw its spear, but Alastar simply caught it, yelled a "Thank you!" and used it to help him balance like a walking stick as he ran.

They reached a river with a small rope bridge, which Donnon cut free so that the remnant trying to cross over were swept away by the river rapids. More tried to follow, but the same thing happened to them.

Alastar stood, catching his breath when finally, one of the remnant got smart and used his spear to stabilize himself as he crossed the river. A quick thrust in the chest with Alastar's spear sent him back into the water, but the two decided to keep on the move, in case others saw what happened and realized how to cross as well, in larger numbers this time.

Alastar and Donnon crossed a swamp and several rocky hillsides before finding themselves on a plateau Donnon recognized as being on the border between his clan's land and that of the neighboring one.

The trail of remnant was long gone, and the two were able to catch a breath of air. Donnon knelt at the nearby stream and cupped his hands to bring water to his mouth, eyes never leaving their surroundings.

After he had his fill, he sat back and pointed to the reflection of the now setting sun, glimmering off of a lake not too far off.

"We'll find Clan Lockmire there," Donnon said, pointing to the far side of the lake, where plumes of smoke could be seen rising from the point where a grouping of trees was nestled between the hills.

"Can we rely on their assistance?"

Donnon shook his head. "Not likely. They're a clan of water mages, and not exactly friendly with my type."

"I'd always assumed the clans fought together in this war." Alastar breathed deep, and Donnon was pleased to feel a gentle warmth come over him a moment later, regenerating his muscles.

"For most of us, there is no war. There's the paladins, murdering our people and those of the other clans. Some would rise against your type—"

"Not my type," Alastar interrupted with a shake of his head. "Not anymore."

"Aye, good. It's about damn time." Donnon shot him a grin. "Their type then. Others hope to wait it out, hope the king of the south will unite these lands as it's rumored this place once was."

"You believe those stories?" Alastar scoffed. "Half of what you hear can't be believed. These lands are full of ghosts, they say, even now. But that's at least explainable, with the underground tunnels and buried cities, and people like Estair and theirs. But the stories of old? Some say there were vampires, werewolves… even visitors from the stars."

"Is that so hard to believe, considering?"

"You mean because we do magic… and aye, I have come to the realization that it's magic. If this is possible, why not the next step? Why not vampires and all that?" Alastar shook his head, staring off at the plumes of smoke. "Sure, and then dragons, next. Maybe we'll meet ourselves one of them someday, and it'll be sitting on a pile of treasure."

Donnon laughed. "Aye, and then we could hire ourselves bands of mercenaries to keep it from the Storm Raiders."

"Or just keep the dragon as a guard-dog instead of killing it."

"You're mad if you think anyone can be friends with a dragon." Donnon laughed.

Alastar turned to him and frowned. "I was only suggesting a hypothetical idea, yet here you are sounding like you believe in those, too."

"When you live in the highlands, you start to believe anything is possible."

"Like a fairy of light coming to our aid." Alastar stood, ready to carry on, and Donnon joined him.

"You learn to do the magic without the fairy," Donnon said. "Or spirits, or whatever. Even hand gestures and other means of summoning a spell, it's all in our minds, really. Some would say I'm crazy for thinking so, but I'm certain."

As they walked down the hill and toward the lake, Donnon glanced up at the sun, wondering how much time they had left.

"I hope you have a plan for following them," he said.

"We're connected, just like me and you are."

Donnon shook his head. "I assure you, the two of us aren't connected in any way."

"The fairy, she took me right to you," Alastar explained. "I have a theory that she'll go to whomever I have a connection with. She led me right to you, and will lead us to Rhona and Kia when I've replenished enough energy to summon her."

"Good," Donnon said, leading the way down through the craggy rocks he'd loved to climb as a child, but now served merely as a hindrance. "They might give us food and offer shelter, but I'd just as soon have Rhona and my Kia back before nightfall. Who knows what those monsters are doing to them."

"We'll have them," Alastar promised. "And when we do, those *monsters* will suffer for this day."

A glance at the former paladin was enough to see that he meant business. His sister was, it would seem, as important to him as Kia was to Donnon. That gave him hope, knowing that the man beside him would fight to his last breath to keep those two safe, just as he would.

And with Alastar's newfound understanding of his magic, there wasn't anyone Donnon would rather have at his side in a fight such as this.

CHAPTER EIGHTEEN

Rhona blinked, looking around to clear the haze from her mind. She had closed her eyes to rest so that her magic would return faster, but must have drifted off to sleep.

Inches from her face, the little girl stared at her with wide, hazelnut-brown eyes.

"Kia… how long was I out?"

The girl leaned back and shrugged. "I can't really tell in here. A minute's like an hour."

"True enough," Rhona admitted as she stretched and stood. She focused and felt her eyes cloud over with black, then smiled. "We're ready."

"How does this work?"

"I haven't the slightest idea." Rhona looked around at the purple glow of the walls, wondering where it was coming from, then went to the door to see if she could see light through the cracks. Nothing. "My best bet? See if we can become shadows and get to the other side of that door, then figure it out from there."

"Won't we get, I don't know, squished?" Kia knelt and looked at the lack of a crack at the base of the door. "Or worse, what if we're trapped there forever as shadows?"

"You ask smart questions for a kid."

"When you grow up in the clans, you gotta grow up fast."

"Nowadays, I imagine that saying holds true for much of the world," Rhona said as she held out her hand for Kia. "Come. If we don't try, we'll never know."

"Kid here," Kia protested, "not exactly worrying about life regrets and what ifs."

"Some kids do," Rhona replied. "I know I did. How about a longing to see your dad?"

Kia frowned and took her hand. "That was a mean way to get me to go along with this. I don't think I like you very much."

"As long as you like me enough to want to get out of here with me, we're good."

It took a moment, but then Kia nodded.

"Great," Rhona said with a laugh. "Just, hold on."

She felt the room darken as her eyes became a deeper black, and then imagined the two of them as shadows moving for the cracks in the door.

Only, nothing happened.

Kia cleared her throat.

"I'm… trying," Rhona protested, and then focused even more.

"Maybe you still don't have the energy?"

Rhona shook her hand and let the girl's hand drop. This wasn't making sense. She tried to feel the shadows around her, to manipulate them, but nothing worked. In the short amount of time during which she had been able to work with these powers, nothing like this had happened before.

The purple glow, she realized, must be related somehow. Something was blocking her powers.

"Let's just hope that your dad and my brother come looking for us soon," she said, shaking her head in disbelief. She had been so certain she was going to get them out of there.

"You're giving up?" Kia turned on her, furious. "You blink a few times and then call it quits? *Damn*, I had a pet cat once that tried harder than you."

A curse coming from the lips of a child somewhat startled Rhona. Childhood in the clan was certainly different than growing up around the Order.

"I'm all for ideas," Rhona said. "Right now, faced with powerful magicians and some sort of spell or something that's blocking my powers, I have to admit that it doesn't look hopeful."

"Blocking your powers," Kia said with a smirk. "*Your,* being the key word there."

"I don't exactly see any flames around here for you to manipulate."

"Yeah, see, smart for a kid again." Kia smiled an arrogant smile that said she knew something Rhona didn't.

"Might as well spit it out then. What is it?"

"Well, I got to thinking while you were passed out. Thing is, your magic doesn't work like ours. I mean, sure, there are shadows everywhere. Even when the sun is at its brightest, shadows are strong. But I think it's not that—I think you're able to pull on your magic *without* the presence of your skill-base. Meaning…" She held out a hand, and suddenly a ball of flame was flickering in its palm. Her eyes went from the flame to Rhona, and creased into a wide smile.

"You practiced that while I was asleep, didn't you?" Rhona asked, voice hushed in awe.

"A little bit. Too rehearsed?"

Rhona ran a hand through her strawberry hair, considering this. "If you can do it, couldn't everyone?"

Kia shrugged. "Maybe, sure. But maybe it's one of those things about believing, right? A nine-year-old finds it easier to believe, and therefore easier to call upon a power that is based on belief."

"I'm not sure if… Well, if I believe you really are nine. Are you serious with all this? I mean, who the hell taught you to think and talk like this?"

The girl laughed. "In the clans, men are the warriors, women raised to be leaders. I've had tutors since I was four who ingrained in me different ways to approach problems. This, as I see it, is simply another problem to be solved."

"Okay, smarty-pants," Rhona said, crossing her arms across her chest and frowning. "Go ahead, show me how you get us out of here."

A hint of doubt crossed Kia's eyes, but then her smile returned, and she said, "Stand back," before pulling back the hand with the flame still coming from it. She then pushed forward, so that a stream of flames poured forth and had the door hinges melting before their eyes.

"Holy… Remind me to tell your dad to teach you how

to be careful with this magic stuff," Rhona whispered, then jumped as the door fell outward with a clang that echoed through the chamber beyond.

A guard came running, but froze in his tracks at the sight of the little girl with flames coming from both hands now.

"Wait," Rhona said, stepping out of the room to join her. "Let me try."

She focused on the powers within again, and then, to her relief, the shadows around the man swayed like trees in a storm. With more confidence, she pushed. This time, the shadows moved over his eyes and mouth, and when he tried to scream, nothing came out.

"Eww," Kia said, glancing up at her. "That's like, one of my worst nightmares. Can't I just burn him to death?"

"Um, no." Rhona twisted her hands, and the shadows twisted around the man and then flung him up to the ceiling, where the shadows there engulfed him.

"What happens to him next?" Kia asked.

"I forgot how kids love to ask questions," Rhona said, rolling her eyes. "Instead of hypothesizing, what'ya say we get out of here?"

Kia shrugged. "I was just curious."

"Well, if your dad says it's okay after we're back with him, we can try it on you, and you can let us know where you go. Deal?"

At that, Kia got squeamish and even lost some color. "Let's just leave it unanswered. I can handle that."

"I bet you can."

Together, they ran down the hall in the direction the

guard had come from, and then up some stairs. As they approached the top step, they heard voices and saw a flickering of light.

Rhona held out a hand and whispered, "Careful with using our powers too quickly. We don't want to be forced to slither out of here on our bellies due to a lack of energy."

The girl simply nodded, not taking her eyes off of the flickering light ahead, and then took another step. Rhona cringed, sure they would be spotted at any second, but when no shouts of alarm rang, she joined Kia. They came upon a landing with a stone floor that circled around a central area that was like a very large column with a door in it, so it was clear this was either another room or possibly a spiral staircase.

Rhona was willing to bet the latter.

A shadow fell across the stones from their left, so they did their best to remain silent as they ran the other way. When they reached the inner wall, they paused, and then slowly starting walking around it, aware of the fact that the voices were moving their way from behind.

"Why don't we just leave and deliver the woman?" a weary voice asked. "Get it over with."

"They say we're waiting on the local High Shadow to arrive," another voice replied. "If he isn't here to make the delivery…"

The voices hushed, too low for Rhona to make out, so she slowed.

"Better to keep them at each other's throats," the first one was saying. "Eventually, they snap. Turn on each other."

"Keep your politics out of it, I say. Far as I'm concerned, we do our job, get paid, and then get the hell out of here."

Rhona paused at the creaking of a door, then heard the voices die off as the other started talking about what he'd do to a woman if he had his share of the pay, before his voice faded away completely.

"You shouldn't hear stuff like that," she said to Kia.

Kia puckered her lips and then nodded. "On one point, we finally agree."

"What do you say to finding out if this is our way out?" Rhona patted the wall behind her. "Get into that stairwell. Run until we see daylight."

"Or the moon," Kia replied. "No windows, hard to tell which it'd be."

"Right, run until we see the sun or the moon." Checking around the bend, Rhona confirmed they were clear and then said, "Now."

They stayed close to the wall in case anyone was around to see them, but it was unnecessary. It was also, Rhona realized as they ran, rather pointless. She had forgotten about the fact that the corrupt mystic was using his powers to somehow sense her if she used her magic. The minute they got into trouble, she would give away their position.

Which made her wonder... why hadn't they already come for her? Suddenly, something felt very wrong.

But for now it was run, or rely on a nine-year-old girl for their defense and escape.

Inside they found stairs, as she had expected, and began their ascent. They came to the next level and opened the door a crack to see just another floor like the one they had come from. The two guards, or whatever they had been, seemed to have left the stairs, but that didn't tell Rhona much. Her best bet, she figured, was to go either all the way to the top, or all the way to the bottom.

Since they had started in darkness, she figured it would be all the way to the top. On and on they ran, but on the fourth floor, Kia had to pause for a breath. They carried on, then Rhona and Kia turned a corner and found themselves in a room with a bed on the far wall, two figures pressed up against the wall near the bed. The man turned to her, his long, blond hair flying out as if hit by a gust of wind, his eyes piercing. The sorcerer Wodain.

The witch at his side frowned at the sight of them, then laughed.

"These are the two you've captured?" the woman said.

"For your information, Elaise, these two are capable of being some of the most powerful users I've ever come across." Wodain turned, pulling his hand from under her dress and letting it fall with a resentful glance before glaring at Rhona. "If they would simply listen to reason."

"Let us go," Rhona said. "She's just a little girl."

Wodain shook his head. "Just… *Just* is such a misused word in that statement." In a flash of white, he was standing a foot away, leering down at Kia. His left eye twitched as he reached out to her chin, his hand froze halfway there, shaking. "You see, I know what she's capable of, as I know what you are capable of. This land, where magic goes unchecked and isn't taught… it's dangerous. It leads to people like the two of you, so different, yet your powers come from the same source as the rest of us. See, I'm the only one who gets it. I'm the only one who knows that, if I could but open up my mind, I could easily do what both of you do. They call me mad, but when we bring you to Her and take your powers for ourselves, they'll all see."

"All we are is a young woman and a girl, trying to be with our loved ones." Rhona glanced over at the witch, mind spinning for a strategy of escape. "You two must understand."

"Because you walked in on us being intimate?" Wodain asked, then laughed. "Do you honestly think I would allow anything other than what I approve in this place?" Again, his eye twitched and, in that second, his expression completely changed to that of a madman, almost like a remnant even. "Don't doubt my powers over you, you pitiful excuse for a witch! I'd have your magic right now if…"

He pulled back, the crazy fading from his eyes. But she had seen it now and was too curious to see where it would lead him to let it fade so fast.

"Ah, but you can't, can you?" She laughed. "They won't let you torture me, or even get into my brain to learn my secrets. You are no better than a slave to them!"

Wodain's eyes went wild again, and he stepped forward, shouting as he raised his hand. In that moment, they were surrounded by walls of flames, bursts of lighting, and more. Until, just as quickly as it had come, the flames and all the rest were gone.

For a moment Rhona couldn't breathe, until she realized he must have been in her mind, and that the flames were fake.

"Don't push me," he said, chest heaving and, once again, hand shaking. He pointed at her with a trembling finger and added, "You think I care about Her and the orders? You think I care?!"

"Wodain!" a voice shouted from the door, and Rhona spun to see Master Irdin there, glaring. "Why is the prisoner out of her cell?"

"How dare you question me?" Wodain said, then stepped forward and, with a sneer, held out his hand as his eyes went white. Master Irdin began to choke, then collapsed to his knees before toppling over to slam facefirst on the floor.

Rhona gasped and pulled Kia close, covering her eyes.

"You see?" Wodain asked. "I am above them all!"

Rhona took Kia by the hand and ran, the sound of cackling laughter echoing behind them. The man was insane, she was sure of that now.

A voice carried after them, as if in their heads, "You can't escape us, not in here."

"No hiding," Rhona replied, feeling at one moment hope slip away, and in the next come surging back with fury. "Not when he can get into our head. But if we were to go there and take care of these clowns once and for all... everyone we know would be safe."

"You do realize you're asking a nine-year-old girl for help in killing others?"

"Well, when you put it like that..."

Kia held a finger in front of her mouth and made a 'Shhh' sound, before setting a flame from the tip of her finger, and then blowing it out with a hint of excitement in her eyes.

"Again, not so sure you're really nine," Rhona said.

"By the way you look at me right now, I'd say you know

I am, and it terrifies you." Kia stood and stared her in the eyes, unblinking. "You wish you could have been half this powerful at my age."

"I don't even want this power I have right now."

"Don't you?"

Rhona felt the little girl's eyes piercing into her. Damn, she was right after all. The power she felt when using magic was the most amazing sensation she had ever experienced.

"Well, let's have some fun, then," she said as she followed Wodain, who appeared again not far off ahead.

He led them through a hall lit with lamps that made it gleam white and then around a corridor that was half-modern, half-polished tiles from the old world. At the other side of the room, he motioned to a door and smiled, then walked right through the wall.

Rhona nearly fell backward in surprise, and Kia let out a squeal.

"Merely a mental projection," the mystic's voice said from all around them. Rhona frowned at Kia and asked, "Is that something other mystics can do?"

"I've never met one."

"Ah, right."

She led the way in through the door, reaching deep down to be ready and pull on her magic should she need it. This little girl at her side didn't belong here, but leaving her back in the dungeon hadn't been an option.

While Rhona was too young still to have her own daughter, she often wondered what it would be like and whether that was in her stars. But most of all, she thought about how, if Kia had been her daughter, how badly she would have fought to keep the girl out of a situation like this.

She wasn't judging Donnon at all—this was, it seemed, Rhona's fault in a weird way. It was more that the guilt of the decision to allow Kia to fight alongside her was eating at her, even though she knew it was their best chance of survival.

They walked farther into the room and saw a table near the far wall. The sorcerer, Master Irdin sat at the head of a sturdy, oak table. He had changed so that he no longer wore the black and purple robes, but instead wore sleek robes of purple and green, with a symbol on the left shoulder of a six-pointed star surrounded by a circle.

Seeing him there made her wonder what had happened in this place so far, and how much of it was real, even now.

He paused from his eating and noticed Rhona staring at the symbol.

"The North Star," he said with a smile, then carefully dabbed at his mouth with a napkin. Oddly, his plate was empty, and the napkin appeared clean. Had he really been eating at all?

"Okay, I'll bite," she replied, "what's the significance of the North Star?"

"A guiding light, a symbol of hope. You'll learn one day, perhaps. But for now, just know that it means I serve a higher purpose, one that you have, until this moment, stood in the way of."

She shook her head, confused. "How's that?"

"You resist when you should succumb. You fight against us when you should be fighting with us, for the greater good."

"If your greater good means dispensing with the lives of people like my brother, or Donnon, or this girl here," she nodded to Kia, who was still standing behind her sheepishly. "That's not something I can allow."

"You mean you're too weak to do what's right." He stood, and unclasped his robes, then let them fall around him so that he was now wearing only his pants. His torso was covered in tattoos of ancient symbols and more, and in their midst, that same six-pointed star. "See that I am devoted, and believe me, if you can find the wisdom to see truth. Sometimes the weak amongst us must be rooted out, but sometimes a new power is born from among the weak. You must often test them to see if the powers emerge. If not, what value do they have to our new society?"

"It wasn't long ago I served one who saw magic users as the ones who should be purged."

"Aye, there are plenty of those, too. A healthy balance of purging to be had for all."

"See, this is why we're going to be on our way."

"Exactly," Kia said, glaring. "But I'd like to purge *him* first."

"Kia…"

"Let the child speak," Master Irdin said, holding up a wrinkled hand. It struck Rhona as odd, as he looked much younger than that hand would lead her to otherwise believe.

Kia held his gaze with eyes fiercer than many grown men Rhona had known.

"What makes you so sure I'm the bad guy here?" Master Irdin asked. "I took you for your own protection, you see. There are those who would cause you harm. Not I."

"Are you insane?" Rhona asked, stepping between the two. "After everything you've done, the people you hurt to get to me, and the remnant you use? Of course, you're evil!"

The room reverberated, an echo of shadows, and Master Irdin smiled.

"You seem to be mistaken, Rhona," he said, ignoring whatever was happening. "How many did you see fall? How many of those that may have fallen did you really know… were truly pure of heart? Any that my people attacked were certainly not the good people you were led to believe, and in truth, we meant to retrieve you from them with haste."

"Retrieve me?" She took another step, the shadows growing darker than dark. "Explain this to me!"

"Your powers are quite unique," he said, gritting his teeth to resist whatever was happening from the darkness and the effect of Rhona's magic. "We've seen the power of light rise up in this land, a power that is truly different from the elemental magic you see among the clans. It truly terrified us, until now… when we believe we have a way to keep it under control."

"And that would be?"

"Light and dark. Two opposites, yet how can you have one without the other? You stand with us against the paladins… those same paladins who still roam these lands and stay strong as we speak, and we may yet be able to quench this light."

"You speak as if you know me, and therefore, I can only assume, you know that my brother is a paladin of the Order of Rodrick."

"Was."

"Excuse me?" Rhona shook her head, trying to make sense of all of this. "Was?"

"Your brother has thrown off his armor, turned against his former brothers in the Order, and now? Now he, too, could very well be welcomed as one of us, if you were to think smart there."

"Why are we listening to him?" Kia asked, turning her glare at Rhona. "He threw us in the dungeons and, before that, led mindless beasts against us all."

Rhona considered this, remembering how, just moments ago, she had been thinking how wise this girl was. Wise beyond her years.

And that made all the difference.

The man before her saw the fury in her eyes as she looked up, and he acted before her magic flared. His hands moved swiftly, ice flaring up around Kia, moving for her heart—but Rhona smiled.

The fool didn't know Kia like she did. He didn't know what she was capable of, and so when she stared with horrified eyes at the oncoming ice while at the same time pushing her hands forward, he was quite surprised when flames appeared around her and pushed through the ice, surging toward him.

Master Irdin froze in confusion, and so Rhona acted. The ripples she felt in the shadows told her she needed to leave immediately. She grabbed Kia and, in the sudden darkness that took over the room and only allowed for her to see, they ran.

"We need to kill him!" Kia shouted as she was pulled along. "He needs to die!"

"It will happen," Rhona said as they ran along dark hallways, "but his reinforcements were too close for comfort, and we aren't yet ready to take them all on yet. Not by ourselves."

Kia stopped resisting and gasped as the lights flickered back on to reveal a door before them. They threw it open and both were amazed to see stairs leading out and down into a castle garden with hedges as tall as walls, fountains scattered among rose bushes, and statues of tall lions and unicorns.

They made their way through, breathing the fresh air and the scent of roses, until they reached the far hedge. A wave of cold air came over them, settling into Rhona's bones and giving her the chills.

Warmth burst forth from Kia's direction, and Rhona turned at the orange glow to see that the girl had a flame in her hand. Kia smiled and twisted it around her hand, then rolled it across her knuckles like an old coin.

"How is one little girl so brave?" Rhona asked.

"My dad's a great teacher."

They shared a smile that quickly faded when Rhona looked around, lost. "We have no idea where we are, or how to get out of here."

"I'm sure you'll figure it out." Kia gave her an encouraging nod.

Even in this dire situation, Rhona couldn't help but laugh. "I'm supposed to be the one comforting you, not the other way around."

"You haven't met that many nine-year-olds, have you? We're tougher than you seem to think."

"I can't argue there."

She held out her hand, and the girl took it while keeping the flame alight in her other hand. Together, they made their way past one hedge after another. At a right turn, they passed a fountain with a statue of a woman standing tall, a staff in her hand and a sword in the other. It was intimidating and so lifelike that it caused Kia to pull back.

"See, I'm not always brave," the girl said.

Rhona squeezed her hand and pulled her past the statue. "Being afraid has nothing to do with being brave."

Walking past a small pond with ducks swimming across its surface, Kia's color returned, and she even paused to watch one of the ducks lift itself up and beat its wings, very uncharacteristically of ducks.

"My mom wasn't a mage," Kia said. "I could always see that she was afraid of it, but that never caused her to look at me or my father any differently. The first time we learned I had the magic, they found me in a field surrounded by flames, crying. She didn't stop to worry about herself or wait to run for help... she ran right through those flames and came for me. She was always there for me like that... always, until she wasn't."

"I'm sorry for your loss," Rhona offered. "My own mother... I wish I could say she was brave. I'd like to imagine she was, but the memories are all a blur."

"You lost your mom, too?"

Rhona nodded. "When I was younger than you, aye." She could feel Kia's eyes on her as she looked away, but offered no more than that as she led them deeper into the hedges.

At first, Rhona thought nothing of the statue. They

passed what she hoped was a replica of the statue a second time, but even then, it wasn't too strange. The clue that something was wrong came when, having nudged a hole in the grass with her boot the second time through, they came to the statue again after going completely straight, and that hole in the grass was there.

"We're going in circles?" Kia offered, eyes wide.

"It might be worse than that."

Rhona closed her eyes and felt the shadows—only they weren't there. None of this was real, she realized with horror.

"Stay close," she said, wrapping her arms around the child. The girl was brave, but how does one explain to a nine-year-old that your escape was no escape at all and that you're somehow trapped in a world conjured up by the magic of a mystic?

Showing her might be the easiest route, so Rhona let the shadows that she could feel, off in the distance, rage. A piercing scream came a moment later, and then everything around them faded.

Instead of the hedges, they were surrounded by walls of stone and brick, glowing purple. Instead of the night sky above, it became very clear that they were still in the dungeon where they had started.

A check showed a power that she guessed to be the mystic was still nearby, but, at least for now, he wouldn't be strong enough to use his magic on them. Unfortunately, Rhona realized as she pitched forward and caught herself on her hands and knees, wanting to vomit with the clenching in her gut, her powers wouldn't be much help either.

"Again?" Kia asked, catching on to the situation quickly.

"If you have it in you, aye."

Kia stepped forward and began applying the fire to the door hinges once again. They couldn't know if it would work this time, or how much of what they had seen the first time was real, but they had to try.

CHAPTER NINETEEN

Water rose up on both sides of the village entrance, forming spirits that looked like men with spears of water. The spirits considered them, but turned their focus on Donnon. Both men lowered their weapons. The spirits nodded, then returned to the moat that surrounded the village walls.

Alastar looked to his companion for advice on what to do here, but Donnon just stared forward, waiting. Finally, the gates opened to reveal a stout woman clad in blue, flowing robes.

"Water magic?" Alastar asked.

Donnon nodded. "And they would've attacked if they judged us to be here for nefarious reasons."

"They know we're not?"

"They suspect we're not, based on my coming here without my clan at my back, I'd imagine."

The woman was walking toward them, hands spread out majestically so that she appeared to be a water spirit herself. Her eyes were fading back from black, a smile forming on her face.

"You, Donnon, are welcome here," the woman said.

"Just like that?"

She smiled, now clasping her hands behind her back. "There was a time when I would've turned you and all fire mages away, but… perhaps you haven't heard?"

"Heard what?" Alastar asked, growing curious, as he peeked past her. All he could see were several others in blue, hands out at the ready should he or Alastar try anything.

"And who is this?"

"He's with me," Donnon replied. "A friend."

Alastar nodded his respect, regretting speaking up before being introduced, but the woman simply nodded back and seemed to move on.

"The Magic Wars are in full effect," she said. "The paladins have begun their siege on the clans, as we've always known they would. Clans that have already been overrun have found our position to regroup and strategize retaliation, so we naturally welcome you to those numbers. But…"

"But?"

"Your companion… He doesn't strike me as a clansman."

"That's because I'm not," Alastar said. "But what I am, even I do not know. A chance for success against them, for one. Donnon's companion, of course. And… a former paladin.

"A *former* paladin?" She scoffed. "Am I wrong in the

knowledge that you are a paladin from your devotion ceremony to death?"

"So the saying goes," he admitted. "Do I believe the
paladins can return to the light? Aye. They don't understand the clans or magic, and so they attack. But I also
know that what they're doing now is wrong. That the war
on magic cannot continue, and that someone has to show
them the error in their ways."

"And that someone would be you?"

"Yes," he said.

"You're lucky we don't require humility to enter these
gates, or you'd be long gone."

Donnon cocked his head. "I'll assume that means you're
letting him enter."

"He's with you, and he seems to speak truthfully, from
his heart." Her eyes narrowed as she lowered her voice.
"But should there be even the slightest thought of betrayal,
he will have the water spirits to answer to."

"You still haven't introduced yourself," Alastar noted. "I
should like to know whose patience I rely on to keep my
life."

She laughed. "Layla, of Clan Lockmire." For the first
time, her eyes softened as she turned them back to
Donnon. "It's been a long time. Gordon will be excited to
see you."

"Excited?" He looked skeptical.

"Well, as much as can be expected," she replied with a
smile that was hiding something. "Go on, you'll find him in
the great hall, tending to the wounded."

They expressed their appreciation and headed on

through the village. Most of it was surrounded by a fence of logs, the tops of which had been carved into points, with rows of sharpened sticks poking through to keep off invaders or straggling wild animals. Huts were built in much the same way, and the rear of the village went right up to the cliffs on one side, surrounded by trees on the other two. Alastar saw why it would be easy to miss if not for the smoke or, unless you were close enough, the enticing scent of cooked lamb.

But his attention was on the interaction between Layla and Donnon, and he had to know.

"What are we walking into with this Gordon business?"

"He was my best friend until they caught us. Introduced me to my wife, may she rest in peace."

"But…?"

"We were of different clans, and they told us we couldn't be in contact anymore. If that hadn't happened, I wouldn't have been surprised if she had ended up with him instead of me. That would've saved me a lot of heartache, but heartache I would never give up for all the world."

"Because of Kia?"

"Her and all the moments shared, all the memories. The statement holds true, you know, about it being better to have loved and lost."

"Yeah, well, paladin here, so…"

"Wait, that rumor about you all taking a vow of abstinence is true?" Donnon burst into laughter. "What the hell'd you do that for?"

"We are required so that we might focus on our duty. Defend the lands."

"From people like me, right?" Donnon chuckled again, but gave him a disappointed shake of the head. "Good job there, buddy. Kept yourself dry so you could fight an enemy that never should have been an enemy to begin with."

"It's not just you all," Alastar countered. "With these new sorcerers, and anyone who disrupts the peace, really, we—"

"So, it's *we* again, is it?" Donnon raised an eyebrow.

Alastar stared, caught in his own words. "I'm not sure I can ever truly not be a paladin. It's everything I believe in. It's honor, duty, justice for the people who can't fight for it by themselves."

"And wars with people like me and my daughter, and now your sister."

"No, it's not." Alastar stood tall, refusing to back down. "It was like that, but I mean to change it. I'll recover the Sword of Light, not because I believe it is truly blessed or whatever, but because I know that the paladins will listen to me if I have it. They will follow me, and we can unite the land, the paladins and the clan warriors, together against the greater threat that has invaded."

"And the vows?"

"A vow is a vow…" Alastar's face was stern.

"It might be, unless the world in which you made that vow changes substantially, or maybe a good enough reason comes along to abandon those vows."

"That wouldn't happen."

Donnon turned to him, then pointed past him and said, "Even for her?"

Alastar's breath froze at the sight of Estair. She was at one of several long tables beneath the trees, where groups were eating from wooden bowls. Her blonde hair fell across her face so that he almost couldn't be certain it was her, but deep down inside, he knew.

Layla stepped up beside Alastar and smiled, following his line of sight. "She arrived with the latest bunch of them. More and more areas are falling to the paladins on the one side, the remnant and the sorcerers on the other."

"We can't stay," Donnon reminded Alastar. "Your sister and my daughter need us."

"I know, just… a moment."

He walked up to the table and was almost upon it when Estair looked up and took him in with wide eyes. At first, her eyes went wide with excitement, then narrowed.

"You're not here with your sister?" she said, setting down her hunk of bread beside her soup and staring at him.

He shook his head. "She's been taken."

Her frown remained a moment longer, then creased into worry and compassion as she stood and ran over to him. She took him in an embrace that he was more than happy to reciprocate, and then kissed him on the lips, right there in front of everyone.

A tingling spread from his lips to his fingertips, caused his chest to flutter, and then almost made him dizzy before he pulled back in alarm. His vows. He couldn't… he shouldn't… He nearly forgot he was surrounded by people, only a couple of whom even seemed to have noticed him.

With a guilty smile, she shrugged and leaned in to whisper, "Might want to go along with it here. Don't want anyone thinking you're one of them."

He was about to respond, though he didn't know what

he would say, when she took him again, pressing her lips against his and slipping her tongue into his mouth.

In that moment, he knew it didn't matter if there had ever been a Saint Rodrick or what the reason was he and his sister could do magic. None of that mattered, because all he could think about was the soft touch of her warm tongue, and the longing to pull her in and have more of her.

His fingers were running through her hair, his other hand caressing her waist, moving up, almost to the side of her breast when—

"Sir," she said, slapping his hand away with a giggle. "We are in public."

A small chorus of laughter rose up from the table nearby, and he turned to see Lokane and several other men he recognized looking up at him.

"They needed that," Estair whispered in his ear, then took his hand and said, "And I need something, too."

He blinked, trying to clear his head and regain his senses, but felt them sleeping. It was only when Donnon intervened by clearing his throat that he remembered himself.

"Yes, right." Alastar stood tall, making sure to glance around at the others nearby. "We have to stop this chaos. We can't stand around doing nothing while—"

"You were hardly doing *nothing*," Lokane said, earning him more snickers.

"Is this really the time to be making jokes?"

"Definitely," Lokane said, standing now, his smile vanishing to reveal harsh lines of sorrow. "Because these men and women have all lost loved ones and need something to distract them, so they don't fall down into their own miserable wells of depression and darkness. You know what I say to that? *Hell. No.*"

A small cheer rose up among those that could hear him.

"They are beatable, make no mistake about that." Lokane nodded to the others now starting to listen. "And I believe this man is going to be one of the key figures in helping us to do so."

"Why him?" one of the men yelled.

"He don't look so special," another chimed in.

Lokane was about to answer, but Alastar held up a hand and said, "I'm not claiming to be some great hero. All I can do is tell you the truth."

"You sure that's wise?" Donnon asked over his shoulder.

With a nod, Alastar continued. "I'm here before you in clothes much like your own, but my usual armor is white and gold." A gasp sounded in the crowd. "That's right… I'm a paladin, or was, and maybe will be again. I don't know, but what I do know is that I'm here because I see the error in the High Paladin's thinking. We should not be fighting each other, we should be united. We should be one force, defending the land against these sorcerers and wandering remnant followers, and standing on the shores to tell Storm Raiders they aren't welcome here. These are our lands, united under the fact that our ancestors lived here before the Age of Madness, and somehow made it work. We are blessed with magic, and yet we've let it tear us apart. And that is *damned* folly."

He stood there in silence, waiting, and soon, several among the crowd were murmuring, nodding in agreement.

"And how do we know you're not a spy of theirs?" a

new voice said, heavy with years of harsh winds and warfare. The speaker stood from where he'd been sitting near a tree behind the crowd. He had wild eyebrows over stark blue eyes, pronounced cheekbones, and a wild mane of hair.

"In times like these, there's only trust," Alastar replied.

"And my word," Donnon said, stepping forward to stand at his side.

"Mine too," Estair said, taking Alastar's arm in hers.

Gordon's stare remained unchanged as he weighed the three, and then a smile crept across his face as he turned back to Donnon. "It's been too long, friend."

The two closed in on each other and met in an embrace, then took a step back and looked each other up and down.

"You've changed," Gordon said with a nod of approval. "Looking stronger than I remember you."

"And you've gained a few inches on me," Donnon replied. "That wasn't supposed to happen."

Gordon laughed. "You always did enjoy being the taller of us, I remember that now. Looks like the tables have turned." He turned to Estair and Alastar as the others half-watched and returned to their food. "I don't know how you two got wrapped up with this guy, but he's trouble, let me tell you."

"We already know," Alastar said. "Trust me."

Donnon nodded and added, "But also more help than you'd imagine."

"Aye, that sounds about right," Gordon said. He just then noticed Layla and thanked her before motioning the other three to follow him. As he led them over to a small stream to drink from, he told them about a time when he and Donnon had slept out under the stars and been attacked by what they thought was a wolf, but it turned out to just be a neighbor's dog that had gotten out. Not many kept the old ways of having pets, but in the clans, it was more common. Especially dogs, since they could warn you about approaching remnant or wild animals.

"Nowadays," Gordon continued, "it's mostly been those damned Storm Raiders we've had to worry about."

"Is it true what they say?" Alastar asked. "That they control the very weathers, arriving in dense fog so that you think you're just as likely to choke on it as be killed by one of their swords?"

"Aye, it's true." Gordon's eyes took on a distant look. "We thought they were the worst of our problems until this war broke out. Their raids were spread out, seldom, but terrifying and deadly." He pointed out a river to the east, on the south of the cliffs. "That one wasn't always there before. It's been redirected for our defense, should we need it."

Alastar imagined a squad of water mages using that river to obliterate invading Storm Raiders and shuddered. Of course, with the invaders' ability to control the weather, it would likely be an even match.

Green grass covered the earth around the stream, and purple flowers were just starting to wilt. Fall wasn't far off, though even this far north, it wasn't like the old ones said from the days before. Their grandparents had passed down stories of intense cold and even something called snow. Alastar breathed in a deep breath of air, enjoying the scent of the flowers on the wind. The air was crisper here at the higher elevation compared to his home in the lowlands, and he wondered what life would have been like here.

For a moment he closed his eyes, trying to call back the light fairy, but he opened them and was let down to see that nothing had come of it. After a bit more rest, he would try again.

When they had their fill of water, Gordon's serious expression returned and he asked how the other two had gotten wrapped up with a paladin on this adventure.

"He threw me in a dungeon," Donnon said with a chuckle. "Who knew that moment would have led to this?"

"I'm not sure I see the humor there," Gordon said with a wary glance in Alastar's direction. "And you?" he asked Estair.

"He came to us in his time of need, as he comes to you now."

"And what help can they give?" Gordon nodded back to the crowd of people around their table. "Them? You think they can form an army right now?"

"They would fight," Estair said. "They would fight to their last breath."

"But that's not what we're asking for," Alastar said. "Simply a place to recover, until we can call on our... er... magic, again."

He couldn't help but notice Gordon's raised eyebrow at his use of the word magic, but ignored it.

"We need the paladin's magic to lead us to his sister and my daughter," Donnon explained.

Gordon's face lit up at the mention of Donnon's daughter. "I'd heard, you know. They told me she had a daughter, and I… well, wanted more than anything to come see you two and meet your daughter."

"Aye, but clan rules." Donnon shook his head, then licked his lips. "If you were to help us save her, you would certainly get the chance to get to know her."

"Can you imagine? A fire mage, a water mage, a paladin, and…."

"Name's Estair, and I'm a fire-mage. I'm the only one known to also be able to heal, and… I'm deadly with a bow and arrow."

"And we can get you set up with a great ax," Gordon said to Donnon. "Assuming that's still your weapon of choice?"

"Was when I was a kid, and is now," Donnon replied. "Too bad I lost the one I had in the battle against the remnant. Whatever you have will do."

"It's settled then. The four of us will set off as soon as we're ready… but where exactly?"

They all turned to Alastar.

"I've been trying to say, we need rest. My… magic… will show us. But it isn't working right now."

"How would your magic show the way?" Gordon asked. "I thought paladins were mostly about healing and granting enhanced fighting abilities, no?"

"He's been visited by a spirit," Donnon said with a smirk.

"Like a wee lad?" Gordon laughed.

"Make fun all you want," Alastar said, waving them off. "But until recently, I didn't even believe this was magic, and considering that my light fairy shows me the way to loved ones, as it did with Donnon here, this works for me."

"I've never heard of a spirit doing that," Gordon admitted. "It could be your magic is a different sort than ours."

"Or it could be that all magic's the same, I'm just learning how to use it differently," Alastar argued.

At a look from Gordon, Donnon explained, "Some of the Arcadian mystics have been teaching their ways around the southern highlands. One of them had this theory that all magic is part of a shared energy, or some hogswash."

"In fact, Estair, have you seen them?" Alastar asked, looking back at the crowd.

She shook her head. "I don't recall seeing where they went, no."

"They were good guys. I hope they made it out safely."

"If I were those mystics," Gordon said, "I'd return to Arcadia, or wherever the hell they were from, as fast as I could. This isn't their war. They shouldn't be here."

"Something tells me it won't be so simple," Estair said. "I saw the looks in their eyes when the fighting broke out back at the Fortress of Stirling, and they certainly enjoy a good fight. Especially, it would seem, when the odds are against them."

"Likely dead then." Gordon glared back at Alastar, who had narrowed his eyes at that comment. "What? It's a simple reality that people who go looking for trouble often find it. There's always someone bigger and stronger out there, or in this case, more magical."

"Based on what we've seen from my sister," Alastar argued, "I don't know."

"Yes, but she'll have to learn to control it, or it might consume her," Donnon said. "And trust me, I'm the last person who would want to see that."

"We get it, Donnon." Estair laughed. "You have heart-shaped eyes for his sister."

"You're one to talk, Ms. Kiss-a-lot over here."

She shrugged. "Told y'all I'd bend this paladin."

"Not break?"

"Why would I want him broken if I mean to have fun with him yet?"

"Um, guys, I'm still right here," Alastar said, raising his hand and waving. "So, can we stop talking about me as if I wasn't here, and as if I were some sex toy?"

"It doesn't count as a sex toy until the toy actually puts out," Gordon said, joining in the fun. "So, paladin…?"

"You all can go stick your heads in each other's arses," Alastar said and returned to the stream for more water.

A moment later a shadow fell over him and then Estair was at his side. He drank his water, wiped his mouth, and then turned to her. To his surprise, she wasn't smiling or seemingly planning some witty or sexual comment. She had a tear in her eye and was staring into the water.

"I'm sorry, I'm not used to this boy-girl thing," he said. "But… is this normally part of it?"

She shook her head and wiped a tear with her forefinger. "Sorry, I know I put on this show, but… it's not all fun and games like it appears."

"Fun and games at my expense," he added, but instantly regretted it when her sad eyes rose up to meet him.

"No, don't feel bad. You're right, after all." She let one of her hands fall into the water and watched as the sun-sparkled stream maneuvered around her fingers. "Too many people I know died back there. I seek comfort, and go about it like a fool. And now this? Crying, really? I'm a fool."

"You're not a fool." He leaned forward and took her hand from the water, holding it in his. "You're a loving woman, one who has needs like everyone else here. Me included. And truthfully? I not only enjoyed that kiss, I loved it. The strongest healing spell might as well be a pile of goat dung for all the good it does compared to one kiss from you."

"Corny," she said with a smile. "But thank you."

Her eyes rose to meet his, wide, glistening in the afternoon sun. Her lips looked so soft, the bottom indenting slightly as she bit it gently.

"If you didn't have your vows…"

"We'd be going at it like bunnies right about now," he said with a laugh.

She laughed, too, but hit him. "Don't tease me."

He caught the hand that hit him, and now, holding both hands, placed them behind his head and leaned in for a kiss. It wasn't even intentional, but seemed all he could do at that moment.

And she turned away, letting the kiss land on her cheek, then another on her neck as he leaned in, causing both of them to fall over with him on top.

"What about your vows?" she asked.

"My vows died the day I left the Order of Rodrick behind to save my sister. They went to hell the moment I accepted that my powers weren't a blessing at all, but some form of magic."

"And now you'd make love to me here under the sun, all those people's eyes on us?" She laughed and pushed him back up, but held him there and then kissed him again. "You said you needed rest, let's get you some rest."

He cocked his head and she nodded, then motioned to one of the huts nearby.

"You mean…?"

"I mean get some sleep," she said, smiling again. "I mean to come with you, and… honestly, you're talking about breaking your vows and moving very fast immediately after. What sort of woman would I be if I allowed that to happen? I want you to be certain, and I want us to take our time with something like this."

He blushed, realizing she was right, and then kissed her hand. "It's just… I've never allowed myself to feel like this before."

"Well, prepare yourself for a wild ride." She cringed. "And no, I didn't mean me… though," she leaned into his ear and whispered, "if and when it does happen, you can be sure it will be wild."

And with that she was up, casting him a last glance over her shoulder as she walked away.

Damn, he thought. His world was turning upside down on him, and it wasn't happening nearly fast enough at that moment. He avoided Donnon's amused stare as he walked by the man, and, after confirming with Layla that the hut would be the one for him to rest in, he found a small bed and made himself comfortable.

As he closed his eyes, he hoped Estair would change her mind and suddenly wake him with the caress of her lips against his, but before he could register disappointment that it wasn't happening, he was asleep.

CHAPTER TWENTY

Rhona and Kia had been through the loop more times than they could count now, each time trying something different, but each time failing. They would blink and be back in the dungeon, painfully aware that they were somehow trapped in the spell of the sorcerer Wodain.

They just sat there on the stone floor, backs to the stone wall, staring without focus.

"Two points give me hope," Rhona said, turning to Kia. "One, it's entirely possible the two of us haven't actually used any magic, that this was all in our minds… and we're still full of energy. I'm not sure they've thought of this."

"Which does us no good if we can't escape," Kia pointed out.

"And that's the second point. Magic wears out the user, right? That's my understanding of it anyway."

"So, when it wears out…" Kia's face lit up with excitement.

"Exactly. That's when we make our move."

"But how will we know."

Rhona smiled. "I can't be certain, but either I've gotten so used to the purple light that I'm not noticing it anymore… or it's gone."

Kia bolted upright, looking around with wide eyes. "How come I didn't notice?"

"You too?"

Kia nodded vigorously as she made for the door.

"Not that way," Rhona said. "Something else crossed my mind while we were in the loops of our minds trying to escape… and it's that I thought I was in control of my magic. In reality, I doubt I could control them. Not to that extent anyway."

"What do we do then?"

"We have to act fast, but first… you need to teach me."

"Teach you? You mean how to use magic?"

Rhona nodded.

"You've gone insane here, is that it?" Kia held her hands to her head, as if trying to pull something out of there. "My dad's been teaching me since I was born, even before he knew if I had magic or not. We have to move, now."

"Not everything, just the basic idea. How is it you call on fire when none's around? None of the others do that."

"I just… I don't know. I guess I thought of it differently, like heat is all around us, the ability to make fire is everywhere, so why not?"

"You see, this is perfect." Rhona stood, too, getting excited. "You're telling me that, because you believed it to be, it was. It all makes so much sense now."

"I'm guessing you're going to waste more time and tell me how."

"Yes! But, just bear with me. I always had my doubts about the paladins' beliefs. When they talked of magic, a passion burned within me. Only, I was against what they stood for. And what do paladins stand for? Or rather, what sort of magic do they use?

"Light."

"Exactly!" She smiled wide, feeling her voice rising in spite of herself. "And so it makes sense that my magic would manifest itself as a control of shadows, or darkness, because I wanted so badly to know magic and was so against the light."

"Holy sh—"

"Language." Rhona held up a finger for another second. "And that's why we're getting out of here."

"What, why? Because I almost swore?"

"Not at all. Because I believe in my powers. Because I believe they're within me, waiting to burst out, and that I can come at those bastards out there with more than they've ever experienced in their whole lives."

"Then let's do it instead of standing around talking, please."

Rhona laughed, and then said, "This might be dangerous. I don't *really* know what I'm doing." She held out a hand, and the girl tentatively took it. "Ready?"

"Oh, my god, aye."

"Good." And with that, she closed her eyes and focused on opening herself up to her powers, unleashing them from the inside.

Nothing happened for a moment, but then Rhona cleared her mind and focused on nothing else, only the magic.

The air rippled and suddenly the shadows exploded outward, breaking down the wall behind them so that there was nothing

"Was that you?" Kia asked, her hand shaking in Rhona's.

"I can't quite control it," Rhona replied. "It's more like I focus on a desire, and somehow that desire is achieved, providing I have enough energy."

"So… aye?"

"So, I think so."

"It's a way out." Kia pulled Rhona forward and the two ran out of the broken wall and into a wasteland of ruins. Usually, Rhona might have thought it odd that this child was leading her, but with the way she was staggering after using magic, it didn't bother her.

"Shite," Rhona said at the sight of it all, only vaguely aware of Kia's glance and comment on watching her language.

In spite of it being dark, the whole area was lit up by various fires surrounded by groups of remnant.

She had never seen anything like this. Their dungeon hadn't been in a castle at all, but some old building with tall, metallic walls and black glass windows. It was broken in places with vines growing over it, but was still the most intact building from the old days that she had ever seen.

Before them lay similar ruins and what seemed like miles of concrete chunks, overturned cars and trucks, a crashed airplane, and more oddities that she had come to know the names of but had rarely seen. Some of it was overgrown like the lands of the Order of Rodrick, but other areas were cleared out.

Unfortunately, they didn't have time to linger and take

in the sights, as the sound of the exploding wall had attracted the attention of the remnant from outside and, judging by the storm clouds beginning to form overhead, at least one of the sorcerers.

"Can I start swearing now?" Kia asked.

"Better to save your breath and run," Rhona replied, ignoring her exhaustion. The two were moving past rubble, torn between watching where they placed their feet to avoid falling on the one side, and watching the oncoming remnant on the other.

"Would it be childish to say I want my daddy right about now?"

"I'd say you're a child, so that's perfectly fine." Rhona helped lift her over a piece of debris that stuck up at an angle with metal sticking out of it. "In fact, I'd love for anyone to be here right now!"

The remnant were slowed by the debris laying all around, but they were certainly closing in.

"Come up with a plan!" Kia shouted as the two ran and slid down a hill.

Rhona screamed out in pain as one of the metal rods sticking out of another block of concrete caught her across the shin, but at least it didn't draw blood. She helped Kia up and looked around frantically.

"If I use my powers and collapse, you can't carry me."

"Got it," Kia said, lifting her hands and preparing to strike. Rhona had to give it to her, the little girl frowning in determination even as her eyes conveyed her fear. "Um, where should I hit?"

"Wait for it," Rhona said, and together they ran for a small structure nearby.

"Now?"

"Not yet, wait until—"

A figure lumbered out of the structure, a tall remnant wearing nothing but rags that hung from his rotting body. The putrid smell of him caught in the wind and was almost enough to make Rhona lose consciousness right there.

Her brother had taught her well, all those years in the castle, so she hefted up a block of concrete as she ran and heaved it with both hands. It clanged against the remnant's arms as he blocked the blow, but he shouted out in pain. It was enough to distract him at least, and cause him to drop the club he held. She scooped it up and struck with all her might.

The blow hit him on the head, a solid impact that sent pain up her forearms. But he just turned to look at her, and leered.

"Now," Rhona muttered.

"What?" Kia asked.

"For the love of the Saint, NOW!"

Kia didn't need to be told a third time. She stepped up to Rhona's side and grabbed her, then closed her eyes and moved a hand in a circle above her head. A wave of flames flew out from the two of them, leaving every remnant within twenty feet writhing in flames on the ground.

The loss of energy was instant, and Kia collapsed into Rhona's arms.

It was dark behind the concrete structure, and that's where Rhona carried the girl. Each step caused aches in Rhona's back and legs, but she pushed on, knowing that if she just made it past the light of the flaming remnant, they could hide, undetected.

That is, she realized, until the mystic, if that's what he was, regained his energy to search them out.

And if she was still here when that happened, she wouldn't be able to use magic without him knowing.

She gulped, realizing that hiding wasn't the answer. The only way out of here was if she gave full control to the magic. It was a gamble, but one she knew she had to take.

Closing her eyes and holding Kia tight to her chest, she ignored the screams of the remnant and the rushing winds from the storm above, even the call of a sorcerer who had spotted her and was suddenly at her side. She ignored the change in the shadows as she sensed him reaching out for her, and then she was gone, one with the night, one with the darkness.

Kia was with her, the two of them moving with the wind, flying almost, and then they saw it in the distance, a light… a faint, beating light. Almost like a heartbeat.

It's him, she realized as the darkness carried them toward it. Everything was spinning, and she realized her magic couldn't hold them much longer. They weren't going to reach her brother, but they at least knew in which direction to find him, and that he was out there.

With a flood of moonlight, the two were flying through the air across a grassy meadow, then hit the ground hard and went rolling.

A thud sounded beside her, and then she, too, hit the side of a hill with a jolt like being woken by a bucket of cold water.

All energy was gone.

The best she could hope for was a turn of her head, where she was able to make out the form of Kia struggling to sit up. A moment later Kia's face was over hers, and she was crying over Rhona, saying they had made it, and, "Thank you."

But as Kia buried her head on Rhona's chest, the storm clouds began to roll in. The winds picked up, and there was no doubt… they had escaped the remnant, but the danger was far from over.

CHAPTER TWENTY-ONE

Laughter woke Alastar, and he saw that it was dark outside of the hut. Several others had laid out bedding and fallen asleep, including Donnon and some strangers.

The door creaked open as Alastar moved quietly into the night, and as he cleared his head, he tried calling on the light fairy again. Nothing.

What if it never returned? He considered a scenario where he would have to wander the lands with the goal of finding his sister, but no clue where to start. The remnant hadn't found the village, at least. That likely meant they either didn't have the intelligence to follow a path, or had obtained what they came for—Rhona—and pulled back.

He was willing to bet it was a bit of both, but mostly the latter.

Several clanspeople around the fire turned as he approached, and Lokane beckoned him over. They scooted to make room, and one of the men handed him a mug.

"The others went to sleep later than you did," Lokane said, clinking his own mug against Alastar's. "I hope we didn't wake you."

"Not at all."

The fire flickered, sending shadows dancing across the others' faces, and one leaned in with a sneer. "It true your type ain't never… you know?" He glanced at the woman by his side who looked like she was about to hit him, and laughed. "What, I'm just curious how a man can make that as a conscious decision. I could never imagine a life without your sweet, sweaty body pressed against mine in the act of—ow, OW!"

She had stood now, hitting him repeatedly, and then shoved him backward off of the log.

"Please excuse my crass husband," she said. "He's an idiot."

"Aren't we all?" Lokane said with a chuckle. "The idiot's name is Luke, and you'll see he's not so bad. At least, after you've told him all your secrets."

Luke was standing now, brushing dirt off his shoulders from where they'd hit the ground. "It's a pleasure," he said with venom in his voice.

"It wasn't he that pushed you," Luke's wife reminded him.

Not knowing what to do in this situation, Alastar simply took a swig from his mug, flinching a bit at the heavy ale.

"I forgot," Lokane said, looking sheepish and reaching back for the mug. "The vows don't allow for ale either, right?"

"Screw 'em," Alastar said, and took another swig. "Thing with vows is, they only make sense until they don't. I think it's time to make some new vows, based on what I've learned recently."

"You wanna vow to serve me to the end of your days?" Luke asked, his playfulness returning. "I accept."

Ignoring the man, Alastar went on. "More along the lines of vowing not to stop until these sorcerers have answered for their crimes. No rest until my sister and Kia are free, and we uncover what larger plot is going on here."

"Aye, that's a vow we can all take," Estair said as she walked up to the fire and wiggled her way onto the log beside him.

"We're not all mages," Luke said. "Not even fighters."

"Ask the sorcerers if that'll matter when they're about to kill you and your family."

Luke's wife frowned, then said, "And if all they wanted was this paladin's sister, what then?"

Alastar shook his head. "They want her for the power she represents. Magic they've never seen before that they think they can harness to control the world. Tell me, when's the last time someone controlled the world through violence without hurting anyone?"

"We've stayed hidden from you folk for many years… what's a hundred more?"

"You don't get it," Estair chimed in on Alastar's side. "This isn't about surviving this lifetime, it's about having a world worth living in for generations to come." She leaned forward, her voice crisp and full of determination. "There was a time before the Age of Madness, or before that, who knows, when these ruins around us were real. There was civilization and, I'd be willing to bet, rule of law. Peace. Prosperity. Call me idealistic, but dammit, I want that and more."

"You're damn right I'll call you idealistic and then some," Luke spat back. "That's a dream! All of that technology stuff is beyond us. People who lived long ago and drove things called buses and lived in buildings called Wallma, or whatever the hell those buildings were for, but not anymore. We get by with what we can, because it's the only option available."

"By the spirits," Estair stood now, her voice rising. "Do you hear yourself? It's only been slightly more than fifty years since the end of the Age of Madness. That's nothing! And how far have we recovered to date? We have homes, castles even. We've come so far in our understanding of magic, magic I might remind you, that our grandparents claim to have had no knowledge about. Where is that coming from, huh? Nowhere? Or, is it just possible, that we're meant for bigger things?"

Luke simply stared back at her, along with the others, and finally, Estair realized this. She cleared her throat, glanced around, and sat.

"Sorry," she said. "I just… get so worked up over this."

"You're not kidding," Alastar said, then stiffened as she leaned against his shoulder.

"When the time comes, you'll all know what to do." She wrapped an arm around his waist and, after a moment, he wrapped an arm around her shoulders.

A couple of the others started mumbling about going to

bed and getting some rest, but Alastar and Estair sat there like that, staring into the flames and watching them dance.

He couldn't imagine how he'd survived this long in life without feeling this sensation of a woman in his arms. But no, it wouldn't have done to have just any woman in his arms. This woman was what made the difference.

He felt her squeeze gently and then noticed her nodding off, and he, too, felt his eyelids growing heavy again. Even though he'd slept all afternoon and part of the evening, he could still sleep more, he was certain.

Through a sleepy haze, he watched the embers flare red and yellow, then turn to black. Except for one little flame that danced at the fire's edge.

A flame with a small face, like a gentle woman, looking up at him, smiling.

The fairy!

He darted up, almost knocking Estair over, but she was up a moment later, and there they both were, shouting in excitement.

"The fairy!" he said.

"The spirit," she shouted. "It's real."

"What's all this?" Donnon asked, running from the hut, followed closely by Gordon. "Holy…"

"It's time," Alastar said. "We must gear up and leave immediately."

The next few minutes were a chaotic dash to throw all their belongings together, while the fairy danced around Alastar, constantly trying to run off, but being pulled back to him as if by an invisible rope.

Gordon led them to the town armory, where Donnon

found himself a great battle-ax, Estair chose fighting knives and a bow and arrow, and Gordon took a broadsword.

"I'm not sure you want it," Gordon said, kneeling to move a rabbit skin cloak from a trunk. When he opened the trunk, there was a set of nearly pristine paladin armor, complete with a cloak. "As you can guess, it wasn't given to us, so if you can get over the means in which we acquired it, it's yours."

"Do you think it wise to travel the lands as a paladin?" Alastar asked.

The others hesitated, looking at each other.

"It might get us out of a tight spot," Estair offered. "If nothing else."

"The remnant might be more intimidated by it," Donnon said, "and the paladins might think twice about attacking if they see one of their own."

Alastar commenced with putting on the armor. He glanced over at the fairy and nodded, then said to the others, "Come, enough time has been wasted. We must be on the move."

The others agreed, and so they walked out in pairs, heading for the gates. Before they could reach them, though, Layla strode out with four horses. Alastar couldn't believe his eyes. He had seen paintings of great knights riding horses, heard tales of the great animals, but they were so rare, he had never seen one in real life.

"Something tells me your mission is more than just to rescue your sister and your daughter," Layla said, addressing Alastar and Donnon in turn. "The water spirits do more than bring us our magic, and at night, I hear their whispers. What you four set out to achieve will be of great service to this world, and my friends here," she patted the flank of the nearest horse, "would like to do their part."

"Where did you even get them?" Alastar asked, unable to hide the awe in his voice.

"The clan leaders brought them, and each agrees this is the time. We don't know what we're up against or what can be achieved here, but we know the time for action is now."

"Then we promise not to fail you," Alastar said. He couldn't help but notice the amused smile from the woman, so added, "What is it?"

"You've never ridden, I assume?"

"Aye, that's correct."

"You're going to be glad you're a healer," she said with a chuckle.

"It can't be that hard."

Donnon clasped him on the shoulder. "Just do as I do, and you'll be fine."

"You know how to ride?" He looked from him to the others, who were staring at him with a mixture of humor and pity. "You all know?"

"If you weren't on our side, we'd have to kill you for letting you in on this," Estair said. "The clans have been trying to breed horses, secretly teaching the warriors from each clan how to ride so that, if and when the time comes, we can ride against our enemies."

"Meaning me and mine."

She nodded slightly. "Though, you're excluded from the equation now, thankfully."

He could feel the rage boiling up inside him as if this was a personal insult, a secret held from him and revealed in a moment of betrayal. But deep down he knew it was really a worry for the men he had called brothers and a fear of riding these animals that he hadn't known still existed.

What had he been taught over and over when it came to fears? Face them, head on.

So, that's what he did. In two quick strides, he was at the side of a tall, white horse. "Thanks for including me on the winning side," he said, and put one armored boot into the stirrup and hefted himself up… and promptly fell onto his back, the wind knocked out of him.

To their credit, the others didn't laugh.

"You really hope to be able to mount her in all that armor?" Gordon asked, leaning over to help him up, while the light fairy danced around as if eager to be on its way.

"Aye," Alastar replied, and this time pulled from deep within so that a slight glow sent his arms tingling with extra strength, and he was able to pull himself up and onto the horse.

Instead of being impressed, however, the others looked horrified.

"What'd I do now?" he asked, checking the saddle to see if he was backward or something. Horse's head in front of him, check. Everything else looked good.

"We've been waiting and waiting for your powers to recover so that we can follow this spirit," Estair explained, "and now you use some of those very same powers to climb a horse?"

Donnon glared at him and mounted a red horse with ease, then pulled her over to Alastar's side. "You put your ego above the safety of my daughter again, and our friendship won't last long."

"I'm supposed to not use magic until we've saved them?" Alastar asked. "Who knows what could happen between now and then."

"Seeing as your magic is the only way to find them," Gordon huffed as he mounted a black horse, "I advise you to learn to rely on us."

Estair was the last to mount. She took the horse from Layla with a nod of appreciation, and mounted with grace. It was white like Alastar's, but with black spots on its hindquarters. She looked so regal sitting there, tall and proud, he almost didn't notice the fairy as it circled once in front of his face and then zipped off toward the hills.

"Hyah!" Gordon shouted, kicking his horse into pursuit.

"After you," Donnon said, his frown from earlier replaced by the sort of smile the thrill of a chase brings.

Estair held her horse at the ready, clearly eager to ride, but waiting for Alastar. He wouldn't let them down, he decided, so repeated what he'd seen Gordon do. Only, the horse slowly started meandering after him.

"Oh, come on!" Alastar said, whipping the reins about in hopes that doing so would push the animal into going faster.

Donnon came alongside him, and Estair went slightly ahead, the two taking turns to watch in confusion as he attempted to get the horse to go faster. They hadn't even put the village behind them, and already it was clear his hips were aching. When he'd gone on another fifty feet like this, he shouted in frustration and turned on Donnon.

"What the hell am I doing wrong?" he demanded.

"It's not like you'll pick it up immediately," Donnon replied. "But since we're in a bit of a rush, you'll have to do your best and suffer through it. Now, do exactly as I say, and we'll be making progress in no time."

Alastar pushed his ego aside and listened diligently, and before long they were even galloping, though, he was certain that each time he rose and fell, the splitting headache quickly forming was going to rip him in half, or the pain in his inner thighs would mean it didn't matter if he broke his vows or not, because nothing down there would ever work again.

"I hear people used to go riding for fun," he called out to Estair as he came up alongside her at a point where the horses had to slow to maneuver between large rocks. "Can't say I understand that one."

"You'll get over the pain, and then you'll see."

"Maybe, but I imagine I'll be too traumatized by that point to remember what fun feels like."

She laughed and gave him a look that almost made him forget the pain of riding. "When we rest, I'll take care of you. Don't you worry."

They cleared the rocks and took off again, that look memorized so that he could focus on it with each thud and shock of pain.

The best he could do was stay focused on the fairy ahead, because anything else just kept bringing him back to the pain. How the hell did people ride these beasts for days on end? He wanted to leap off and run the whole way, but running in his armor wasn't likely to happen, and he had no idea how far they would be traveling.

And something was happening as he watched the fairy. Pain seemed to subside, and his energy returned slightly. It wasn't like a full on healing spell, but keeping his focus on the fairy was definitely giving him some form of rejuvenation. He supposed it made sense, in a strange, magical way. If he was pulling on energy, whether it was a great pot or some form of various colors, as the mystics had described the possible ways it worked, then this fairy was just one more way of manifesting his magic. She wasn't a real fairy, in that sense, but a being he created to lead him to people he had a connection with. As an added bonus, she seemed to provide some form of healing.

The real question was how long she would last.

Riding in the dead of night was a challenge, but the horses largely controlled themselves, and the moon and stars were bright. At a dip in a valley, they found themselves descending into a dense fog, then wading across a shallow swamp as they led their frightened horses.

Alastar enjoyed the break from riding and wondered if the aching in his inner thighs would be with him forever.

The fairy was growing dim, and he knew it wouldn't be long.

"We have to move faster," he said as they reached solid land and a spot where the fog was sparse.

Donnon found a hunk of bread and dried apricots in his horse's saddle bag and shared it with the others. "We'll gather our strength, then set off again."

"We have no idea how long it could be," Estair added, seeing the look on Alastar's face. "And arriving without the ability to fight would mean losing before really starting."

Alastar didn't like it, but he took a bite nonetheless. When he swallowed, he was surprised to see the fairy brighten up.

"You see," Donnon said with a nod toward the fairy, "you need the energy boost, too."

"If it'll help us win," Alastar replied as he eyed the increasingly bright fairy.

Estair approached and adjusted his saddle, glancing his way more than once. "You're holding up well."

"I feel like death," he replied.

"The feeling… it goes away."

"You mean the pain?" He cracked his neck. "I have a hard time believing it."

"The physical, aye. But the emotional as well." She took a swig from her water skin and then held it out, offering a drink. He took it and sighed with relief after the cool water had met his dry mouth.

"Living out with the clans?" he asked, handing the water skin back. "I imagine you know something of this."

"Aye." She took the water skin, but didn't put it away. She clutched it next to her chest, her eyes staring off into the night sky. "It's not always against the paladins, our struggles. My brother was lost in a skirmish with another clan, long ago. The skirmish was north, along the great River of Enid. They have a fortress built there to control the mouth of the river, and another clan had asked for our help in taking it. Fool brother that he was, he ran off to join in the fighting. The last I saw of him was when he ran off, carrying his sword above his head and shouting battle cries like the rest of them."

"That's… I'm sorry."

"Wars here, battles… it all seems so pointless. One day it's other clans, the next Storm Raiders, then the remnant, and now these strange sorcerers show up. Will it ever end?"

He turned to see the fairy dancing in the fog, floating around like she was swimming and having the time of her life. "I have a strange feeling… One that tells me we will be the ones to bring it to an end."

She smiled as she took his hand and squeezed. "Damn right we will."

CHAPTER TWENTY-TWO

Donnon's ears perked up and he paused, mid-step as he was about to remount his horse. He had sensed something, and now he was listening… waiting.

There it was again, a gust of wind, followed by a distant shout. The fog was still thick around them, but when he looked to the sky, he saw heavy clouds forming, circling around a point not far to the northwest of them.

But what really caught his attention was when Alastar's fairy of light leapt up and darted off in that direction faster than the others could follow.

"ALASTAR!" he shouted and was already on his horse and riding before the others had a chance to respond. If there was a chance his daughter was nearby, he meant to make sure she knew daddy was here to protect her.

Curses sounded from behind and soon the sounds of galloping horses, and then, ahead of them, the fog cleared as a sudden burst of light exploded in the night.

A man was cursing, and in the remaining light, Donnon

had no doubt that this was one of the sorcerers. He leapt from the horse, pulling free his battle ax as he did so, and landed with a chop that split the sorcerer's head in two.

The twang of arrows sounded nearby, whistling close and then nearly finding their mark before a gust of wind flung them aside.

What remained of the fairy was now like a thousand glittering stars, falling around them like snow.

"How…?" Donnon asked, but then a sound came from behind him, the whimper of a voice that said, "Dad," and Donnon's only thought was to reach his little girl. He plowed through the sorcerer, only distantly aware of a flame that shot toward the man at the same time from somewhere behind him, and then was at her side, his Kia.

"Darling," he said, grabbing her with one arm and wielding the ax with the other, prepared for any attack that might come. "They didn't hurt you, did they?"

"Not yet," a woman's voice said, and when he looked down, he wasn't holding his daughter at all, but a witch. Around her pointed teeth, the white paint on her skin cracked even as she stared at him. Her eyes went black as fire rose from her fingertips.

She cackled, and then was on him, clawing, pulling him into her with hands that burned.

To be so close, he had thought, and then lose his daughter again, was more than Donnon could handle. With a shout of madness, he thrust her off and swung with all his might, again and again, a wild man with a mission in the night.

If Donnon hadn't ridden off without them, Alastar thought, they would have been able to attack whatever lay out there together. Instead, there had been an explosion of light, and he now heard Donnon grunting and cursing, but was still too far back to know what was happening. He pushed the horse harder and now, for the first time, brought her into a real gallop.

Estair shouted for him to hurry, and then a flame lit up the night and fire shot out, followed by more.

And then he was upon them, nearly riding past them as he pulled the horse to a stop and leaped down. He pulled out his sword, ready, and then saw the fight with the witch, a sorcerer dead on the ground, and the swirling storm above.

They are here, he realized. His sister and Kia were nearby, but the sorcerers didn't know where!

"Stay out of sight!" he shouted into the darkness, hoping they could hear him, and then he charged.

The witch had just lifted Donnon into the air with a spell, and she was moving her hands in a motion as if pulling him apart. Her screams filled the air, but were cut short by Alastar's sword coming up and out through the witch's mouth. As he pulled the sword out, she fell to the ground, dead, and Donnon dropped to safety.

"Dad!" a shout came from a hill nearby, and Alastar turned to see a small form silhouetted in the darkness, running for them.

"No, stay hidden!" he shouted, but it was too late.

With a crack of lightning another sorcerer appeared, and behind him, Wodain with his blond hair and white eyes.

"You found us," Master Irdin said. "Or is it that we found you?"

Alastar frowned, debating his next move, and then smiled at a sight—another form rising out of the darkness behind Kia. He knew her form anywhere, and he especially knew the darkness swirling around her, though the circles of purple glowing from her hands were new.

He gripped his sword and focused his energy on her, hoping to heal whatever of her he could, if she needed it.

The fight had come too soon, Rhona knew it, but somehow her powers were responding to the situation instead of waiting for her to recuperate. She was barely even aware that she had stood, and completely confused about the purple light coming from her hands.

Ahead of her, she saw several forms—her enemies, as she had suspected, but Alastar and others as well.

Then, the strangest sensation swept over her as specks of gold appeared in the purple circles around her hands. A glance showed her golden, glowing eyes, and she realized it must be Alastar healing her.

But it was more than just healing, it was awakening. As long as he was doing that while her magic was active, she could feel it coursing through her as if it were simply another layer of muscles she had to clench. She could understand it like it was part of her mind she had never used but was suddenly active, and all she had to do was will an action to be so, and it would be.

So that's exactly what she did. She stepped forward and thrust outward with her spell, blocking spears of ice and causing them to simply vanish into the shadows.

She pulled the darkness around herself like a cloak and flew forward, pulling it with her as she went and then sending it like serpents of darkness to coil around her enemies and squeeze, sucking the life from them.

"You can still stop this!" Master Irdin said, pulling on the spinning circles of ice to keep the darkness away from him. "I'm but one arm of a many armed god. Join us and you can conquer the world, live alongside us as legends!"

She sneered and clenched her fist, watching the darkness push in against him and his magic. Ice formed a bubble around him, shifting and exploding, even sparking, and pushing the darkness back, but it was losing the struggle, and Master Irdin's eyes showed he knew it.

"Come with me!" he shouted. "This is your last chance!"

"The only place you're going is to hell," she replied, and then glanced around to see her brother standing at the ready, Donnon holding his daughter, and Estair and the stranger nearby.

She needed more information so that they could continue the journey and end it once and for all. So she loosened her grip and said, "I will be a goddess among you."

Master Irdin's eyes lit up, although maintaining a level of skepticism. "You will indeed. The High Queen will determine your place, but if you join me, allow me to speak on your behalf..."

"If I accept this," she said, "What happens next?"

"We conquer. With you or without, the Holy Scourge will see these and all of the other lands purged. We will pull all under our rule, control all magic, and make the world a better place for those of us with the gift."

"You disgust me," she spat it out like venom.

"What the hell did you say to me?" His voice quivered with rage.

"How you can sit there and talk about suppressing and killing others, without the slightest hint of remorse in your voice… it sickens me."

"That's what we do, birdy," Wodain said, stepping forward and letting his eyes turn white. "You're nothing to stand in our way. Nothing!"

"NOW!" Rhona shouted, and all hell broke loose at that moment. She gave herself over to the shadows, but again Alastar's healing gave her control, and she was able to press the attack against the evil mystic, fighting back his powers. Donnon and Gordon were calling on fire and water, respectively and pursuing the attack, while Estair took to the traditional approach and shot arrows.

***

Rhona knew Alastar's focus was completely on keeping his healing powers on her so that he couldn't divert his attention elsewhere. The others were doing their best against another sorcerer who had shown up, battling Donnon with fire, but mostly, it was Master Irdin pushing with ice, only Rhona's shadows catching the magic and making it vanish into the darkness before finding their marks.

"You all are like children playing with powers you don't

understand!" Master Irdin shouted as he twisted his hands, and the volume of his attacks doubled.

"Then it's going to be pretty damn embarrassing for you when we kick your arse," Gordon shouted, catching a wave of ice and turning it into water before hurling it back at them in a torrent that tossed one sorcerer to the ground and disrupted a fire attack.

Master Irdin shouted in frustration and stepped forward again, forming a complicated pattern with his hands before him and closing his eyes. Winds howled, and the sky turned red and purple as clouds of ice swirled above their heads, but Rhona and her friends stepped forward, all in a line, prepared to counter his attack. As one, they pushed forward with their war cry, and the magic spells met and clashed in the middle.

Rhona was using all of her power, everything in her with the help of Alastar's magic to give her focus, while at her side, Estair, Donnon, Gordon, and even Kia focused, all eyes clouded over as their hands moved in circles and magic flowed from their bodies. They were giving it their all, and still, this sorcerer managed to hold them off, the opposing magics crashing in the middle, seeming to tear a door between their world and some other dimension.

Then it all went silent, and for a moment, it seemed they would all be dead, and none of it would matter anymore.

With a bang that threw them all back onto their butts, magic exploded all about them, scorching the grass and trees and, at the same time, covering everything in ice. Parts of the ground vanished, eaten up by shadow.

Wodain pushed himself up, staring at it all in horror,

and then his eyes went white. The land vanished, and in its place lakes of flame rose up, spirits like demons surging upward for the attack.

But Alastar was there, ready. He closed his eyes to ignore all of this and charged forward.

For an instant, his fairy of light appeared again, guiding his sword, and then it found its mark. The blade impaled the evil mystic through the chest, and the fire and demons vanished as the man's eyes returned to normal. He collapsed to the ground, eyes fading to a dark gray as he stared blankly into the sky.

Master Irdin stumbled forward, clearly drained from his use of magic. Rhona was glad to see he wasn't as invincible and all powerful as he appeared to be.

Alastar pulled his sword free and pushed himself up. Rhona found her footing, stumbled slightly, but regained her footing and stayed focused on Master Irdin. Gordon and Estair were there, too, all advancing.

Master Irdin's eyes darted to each of them, then to his dead mystic and witch, along with the dead sorcerer at the edge of their fight.

"This won't be the end," he said, his mouth frothing and eyes going wild. "We're too strong for even you, and when the wave crashes down upon you, this day will be the day you'll look back on and wish you'd met death."

Rhona led the charge, but with a fluid motion, Master Irdin lifted his hands into the air, and the last of his sorcerers appeared at his side and grabbed his arm. As his eyes turned black and a crack of wind flared their robes out behind them, the two vanished.

Alastar's sword found empty space, and he shouted.

Rhona spun, searching for any sign of them, but the others stood, chests heaving, and Donnon held his daughter close as a smile crept across his face.

"They're gone," Donnon said. "Maybe just for now, but today… we've won."

CHAPTER TWENTY-THREE

"The remnant still roam our lands," Rhona said. She stumbled over to Kia, resting a hand on her back and leaning against Donnon to rest her head on his shoulder. "And who knows when Master Irdin, or this bigger power he speaks of, will return."

"After the skills I just saw," Donnon squeezed her hand, "I'd have to say that they'll have a fight ahead of 'em if they show their faces here."

"Damn right," Rhona said with an exhausted laugh.

"The remnant will be in a frenzy, I'd reckon," Estair said. "And whatever force the sorcerer talked about, part of some dark society or whatever it was… It's going to push us to our limits."

Alastar sheathed his sword, hands still trembling from the excitement of the fight. "When they return, we'll be ready."

"How can you be so sure?" Rhona asked, familiar with that look in his eyes that meant he had a plan.

"We're going after the Sword of Light, so that the

paladins will unite under me. When the King of Gulanri lends his support, there might be an alliance with the clans. When the Lost Isles stand united, no force will pose a threat."

"It's settled then," Estair said, and to Rhona's surprise, the lady wrapped her arms around Alastar, and they kissed. That deserved some questions, but these were the type of questions that could wait.

Gordon cleared his throat. "The people of Roneland need to know."

"What?"

"They have to be told what's coming, so they can prepare," Gordon continued. "We must return and warn them. At least, some of us."

"Including me and my daughter," Donnon said. When Rhona turned to him, he averted his gaze for a moment, then turned back to her with determination.

"What do you mean?" Rhona asked.

"I only just got my Kia back," he said, squeezing his daughter tight. "I'm in no position to take her to Sair Talem, and could never live with myself if I left her behind."

Everything in Rhona made her want to argue with him, especially the part that longed to have his arms around her, comforting her at night before drifting off to sleep. But instead, she said, "You'll be here when we come back?"

"I'll rally the clans, set up defenses, and protect my daughter."

"I don't need protection," Kia said. But she held tight to him and didn't argue further.

Rhona bit her lip in frustration, but then leaned in and

kissed him on the cheek, before looking at the others and nodding.

"We'll all ride back," she said. "It wasn't so far, and we must ensure you arrive safely. We'll regroup, stock up for the longer journey, and then set off for Sair Talem."

She turned to Alastar, expecting him to protest and insist that they head off now, but he simply nodded.

"It's settled then," she said. "For the protection of our lands."

"For the protection of the Lost Isles, and the lands beyond," Estair said.

Gordon nodded, and Alastar clumsily climbed onto his white horse. Rhona joined him, and Kia rode with her father. Soon, they were on their way back to Layla and the village of Clan Lockmire.

It was quite different, riding on a horse and watching the sun rise over the hills to the east. Soon, the green, rolling hills went from nearly black to being scattered with long shadows and a glow of orange.

"Where did you learn to ride, brother?" she asked as he clucked his tongue and maneuvered the horse to turn toward the village gates.

He laughed. "Oh, this horse is guiding us more than anything else. She's being kind, for the first time this night."

Rhona patted the horse's flank and said, "Good girl. Maybe she just likes me more than she likes you?"

"You know," Alastar grumbled, "I don't doubt that in the slightest."

They soon found the one called Layla, and introduced Rhona. They passed off the horses, briefly telling her what all had happened, and then she showed them to rooms where they could sleep.

"You understand, don't you?" Donnon asked, holding his daughter close as they turned to follow the path to their hut. "I... I'll be setting up defenses, and waiting for you. But if you don't want to go, if you'd rather stay here...?"

Kia looked up at her, that same look of hope that was in her father's eyes, but Rhona shook her head.

"My brother will need me," she said. "If my magic is as powerful as you all keep telling me, then the people of the Lost Isles need me."

He nodded. "I know. But I'll miss you."

Kia ran forward and threw her arms around Rhona, burying her face in her shirt. "Hurry back."

Rhona pulled her back and tilted the girl's chin up. "I will. Your father's a great man, he'll protect you."

Kia laughed. "Or I'll protect him."

"Or we'll protect each other," Donnon said, joining the two for another hug. Rhona was going to miss them, but at the same time, she thought it was nice to have someone to come back to and a reason to fight. She was going to do damn well everything in her power to bring this land to peace.

Alastar curled up in his bed, mind racing with the thoughts of everything he and Rhona had been through in such a short amount of time. They would never be the same, that was certain.

He rolled over, ready to close his eyes, when a form

startled him. His hand shot out for his sword, but the figure leaped through the darkness, caught him by the wrist, and then lunged forward to press her lips to his mouth.

When she pulled back, he could see by the slight golden glow in his startled eyes that it was Estair. The light added shadows that made her lips appear even more tempting than usual.

"You nearly caused my heart to explode," he said, sighing with relief to see her.

"Is that a corny romantic thing to say, or… like literally?" she asked, pushing him back onto the bed and straddling him.

"I meant it literally, but now that you mention it…"

She put a finger to his lips. "Shhh, I don't like corny."

He grinned and was about to make a corny joke, when she leaned in and kissed him again, hips pressing into his, and she took his wrists and held them beside his head.

"You sure you're ready for this?" she asked, pausing with her lower lip barely brushing against his.

He hesitated, falling back to that place where he felt comfortable. He had taken his vows, but then again…

"We're about to ride off to an island known for its ghosts, covered in remnant, all so that we can find a mystical item no one has found before. Then we'll ride back to try and unite the lands against an army of sorcerers and who knows what. Yet, in spite of all that, lying here with you on top of me is the most terrifying of all."

She laughed and leaned in, her warm breath tickling the side of his neck, and whispered, "I'll take that as a very weird *aye*."

His eyes went wide as her lips met his again, and then he wrapped his arms around her, running one hand through her hair as he lost himself in the moment.

If the rest of their journey was going to be anything like this, he couldn't wait.

AUTHOR NOTES - JUSTIN SLOAN

My love of fantasy books dates back to my mother reading The Hobbit to me as a child, then later when I drew and wrote my own comics (fantasy) when I was ten. My love of magic was burning strong then, and it has only been fed more fuel as the years went on.

Now I am able to be part of the biggest thing to hit the market ever--I hope. The Age of Magic is a series that started with Michael Anderle partnering with CM Raymond and Lee Barbant. They created the Rise of Magic books within the Age of Magic, and since invited authors such as PT Hytlon, Brandon Barr, and me (among others) to write in this world. I mention these two named because I am a huge fan of both of their other fantasy series, and have been reading their Age of Magic books and LOVING them.

These are going to be fun books, some approaching a different part of this world, some crossing over, and some with spinoff characters from others. And what else is cool -- they're all part of the Kurtherian Gambit Universe

(KGU), along with my other KGU series, Reclaiming Honor.

I read the first books in this new magic series and loved them. When approaching the idea of what I could contribute, I thought it would be a lot of fun to explore what used to be the UK, especially the Scotland area, but in this world FAR FAR FAR in the future, where magic exists and so much has changed, it's almost unrecognizable. Why here? One reason is that my great grandparents came over to the US from Scotland, and I used to play the bagpipes. That should be enough! But also because I just love this area. I did a short story about King Arthur as a vampire, and hope to develop that into a series someday, but in the meantime want to write more about this area and have an excuse to do research. Also, my other fantasy series took place in an area very similar to Ancient Greece, so I thought it would be great to have a series in a much more typical fantasy setting.

But most of all, these books are about characters for me. And I love Rhona and Alastar. I hope you're with me on this, because I have a lot more of them coming. You'll also see some cool connections to the books PT is doing (pay attention to those Storm Raiders mentioned several times in this book -- they'll come into play, I promise). So be sure to go grab his book (and the rest).

A huge thanks to Michael Anderle, CM Raymond, and Lee Barbant. It's going to be a blast, and I'm so happy these guys will be there for the ride.

AUTHOR NOTES - MICHAEL ANDERLE

MAY 19, 2017

First, thank you for blessing us by reading this book and NOW you are reading these author notes as well!

I'm going to riff off of Justin's author notes a bit when I say that my first memory isn't the Hobbit (that was much later) but rather Dungeon's and Dragons.

And Magic Users!

I have to admit that I HATED the fact that my magic user could only roll 1d4 (1-4) points of health, couldn't wear decent armor and was basically a wimp. I wanted my magic user to be BAD ASS, but no amount of playing fast and loose with the rules really allowed me to roll a new, bad ass magic user.

It truly sucked.

Mind you I understand the why of it right now, but it doesn't appeal to me to roll up a wimpy-dimpy person to this day.

I guess I'll just have to write my own series where we skip that part. Just ask the local Dungeon Master to hand me that level 15 character and some gold and we will call it good.

Then, World Of Warcraft happened a decade ago and they fixed that slow rise to becoming more powerful and it only took grinding through a computer game to do it.

I was HOOKED.

Then life happened, kids and other things and I quit WOW (World of Warcraft) but I never quit loving fantasy. When I worked with LE Barbant (he is the world guy for the team of CM Raymond and LE Barbant) to explain how the Age of Magic was going to work, we had a blast working out the science behind the magic. It is predicated on two concepts:

1) Arthur C. Clarke's 3rd Law - Any sufficiently advanced technology is indistinguishable from magic.

2) $E=MC^2$ - Although there are a LOT of ways of explaining this, it boils down that energy is equal to the mass of an object (matter) and C^2 is the proportionality constant, equal to the speed of light in a vacuum squared.

At the end of all of this wonderful sciency stuff, many of the humans (read most) don't realize that their magical powers are a construct of the Kurtherian Nanites infused in their bodies, now.

At the end of all of these stories (Age of Magic and Age of Expansion), we will have a final Kurtherian showdown and those Kurtherians millennia ago are going to find out what happens when you give Humans abilities they should never have.

I hope we do you, the readers, justice.

Now, this Author is going back to writing my next

Michael Book. I'm about 8 chapters from completion, and hope the fans enjoy it!

Thank you SO MUCH for trying out our stories, and making our lives changed from your input, your support and your reading.

Michael Anderle

JUSTIN SLOAN SOCIAL

For a chance to see ALL of Justin's different Book Series Check out his website below!

Website: http://JustinSloanAuthor.com

Email List: http://JustinSloanAuthor.com/Newsletter

Facebook Here: https://www.facebook.com/ JustinSloanAuthor